The Loved
and the Unloved

To Buzz and Donna:
    with very special
        good wishes

        Hal Phillips

Books by Thomas Hal Phillips

THE BITTERWEED PATH

THE GOLDEN LIE

SEARCH FOR A HERO

KANGAROO HOLLOW

THE LOVED AND THE UNLOVED

The Loved
and the Unloved

by THOMAS HAL PHILLIPS

BANNER BOOKS   UNIVERSITY PRESS OF MISSISSIPPI

Jackson

First published in 1955 by Harper & Brothers
Copyright © 1998 by Thomas Hal Phillips
All rights reserved
Manufactured in the United States of America
01 00 99 98   4 3 2 1
The paper in this book meets the guidelines for permanence and
durability of the Committee on Production Guidelines for Book
Longevity of the Council on Library Resources.

Phillips, Thomas Hal, 1922-
    The loved and the unloved / by Thomas Hal Phillips.
        p.   cm.
    ISBN 1-57806-056-7 (alk. paper)
    I. Title.
PS3566.H524L68   1998
813'.54—DC21   97-42205
                                                         CIP

British Library Cataloging-in-Publication data available

Prologue

EARLY in March, in the year following World War II, the State's executioner was directed to appear in a small agricultural town where a prisoner was condemned to die in the portable electric chair. According to the laws of the State regarding such cases, the chair would be installed, inspected, and pronounced ready at least forty-eight hours before the time set for the execution.

William Morgan was the name of the executioner, and if, in that early March time, he had proceeded with his duties as prescribed by law and custom, it is likely that few people in the State would remember him. As it happened, he became famous for not doing his job.

He brought the chair to the town of Cross City three days before the appointed day. It was installed, but it was neither inspected nor pronounced ready that afternoon. The executioner left the town hurriedly and when he reached home he was in a bad humor. He told his wife the unseasonably bright sunshine had given him a violent headache. He took a bath and went to bed early, something he had not done for years. Usually he was up until eleven or later and did not arise in the mornings until eight or nine o'clock, excepting, of course, the days of execution.

He was actually a kind-hearted person, with many of the ministerial qualities, and for twenty-three years he had been somewhat horrified by the position he held. Yet, he liked his job very much. Once when repercussions from a Governor's race had endangered his position, he went to great lengths to smooth over the trouble: that is, he made several trips to the State capital, and secured affidavits from neighbors stating that he had openly supported the winning candidate.

William Morgan was born on a farm, and by the time he was nine years old he had quit school and taken his place as a grown worker alongside his older brothers. He was inclined to be fat and slow—after the Seaforths not the Morgans— and in the summertime his feet would become scalded and peel to the raw. He vowed to himself that he would one day have a job which would require no walking at all, and such was the epitome of his ambitions.

At eighteen he left home and after a few years as plumber, electrician, carpenter, he finally settled as bookkeeper for a large cotton gin.

The owner of the gin was a politician, a former state senator, whose holdings were large and whose debts were larger. When one of his daughters decided to marry William Morgan, he neither approved nor disapproved, for he neither liked nor disliked William Morgan. Besides, his daughter Clyde was twenty-seven years old and, in his eyes, approaching the spinster age. So he gave her away in the local church on a day in June, and in August, in the Democratic primaries, his candidate won the office of Governor of the State. Fifteen days after the Governor took office, he appointed William Morgan, whom he had never heard of, as the State's executioner.

William was twenty-eight at the time and had not yet reached what he later called the "raw bone stage of living." He was so upset by the appointment that he went to bed for a week. The news had come like a thunderbolt. He had asked for nothing. He was perfectly satisfied to go on as bookkeeper, which was not only seasonal but also a sitting-down job. But after a few months he began to appreciate what his father-in-law had done. On the third day of every month, unless a Sunday or holiday interfered, he received a check for two hundred dollars. That happened seventeen times before he was called upon to act officially.

By that time he was somewhat seasoned mentally. He performed, rather well he thought, and the next day he went rabbit hunting with two neighbors. Each time he shot a rabbit he expected some peculiar reaction to seize him, paralyze his limbs or his mental faculties, but nothing extraordinary happened. It was after all rather hard to look at a rabbit and see the face of a man.

Three days after that first execution, however, he woke up with a violent headache. He remembered that he had dreamed about the dead man and had felt electric charges

in the form of silver arrows pierce his own skull. He turned
to his wife and said, "Clyde, did I sleep well last night?"

She, who was a heavy sleeper, answered, "What a silly
thing to ask me."

"What I meant was, did I keep you from sleeping?"

"I don't reckon you did," she said.

When he got up and moved about, his headache was more
severe than ever. His cheeks felt hot and water dripped from
his armpits. But he was determined not to go to bed. At nine
o'clock he went to the post office which stood between the
cotton gin and one of the three village stores. The post
office was not yet open, or rather, the mail had not yet arrived, and so he went into the store where the idle always
gathered. Every eye turned to him, every head nodded to
some extent; and at that moment he felt a very strange sense
of power. He went to the storekeeper and bought a box of
shells, which he did not really need. Going out of the store,
he noticed that the pain in his head was less severe.

He did not open his mail until he got home, though he
was immediately curious about a letter from the State capital.
The letter, he guessed, would be another of those official
forms which he had had to sign after the execution. Therefore, he was momentarily frightened when a thousand-dollar
check fell out into his hands. The letter began, "In accord-
ance with House Bill No. 92-118 of the Fifty-first General
Session of the Legislature . . ." He sat and marveled for

quite a while. No one had told him there would be a considerable bonus.

After a few minutes, when he felt better, he went to the kitchen where his wife was cooking dinner and asked her if she knew about the bonus. She answered that she did know. But he did not believe her and so he asked, "Well, how much is it then?"

"I don't know exactly, but I've heard Papa say . . ."

"A hundred dollars?" he asked.

"More! You can't kill a man for nothing. I'd think it ought to be a lot more!"

"You'd *think?*"

He had been slow all his life and so was not at all prepared for the sudden action that followed. She dropped a spoon and a dish towel and whirled on him; she seized the letter and the check before he could move a finger; she let out a wild, laughing scream which seemed to take his head right off his shoulders.

"Can you imagine?" she cried.

"Hush, hush," he said weakly.

"Imagine!" she cried again.

He sat down at the cook table. He dropped his head, and when his forehead touched the cool table he realized clearly that every tinge of pain was gone. He felt nothing, absolutely nothing.

During twenty-three years there were nineteen such checks, each bearing in the upper right-hand corner a huge black

star, and in the lower left-hand corner the name of the executed. From first to last, he remembered each name in full,
the age, the crime, the day and hour of the execution. He
kept a notebook, a black one, in which he put down various
items concerning his victims. He allowed several pages
for each one because his notes and accounts were never
continuous compositions, but haphazard bits set down at
random. Sometimes he would remember an item after three
or four years, and so would turn back the pages of his black
book and record the item as if it had occurred the day before.
For that reason, the earlier pages of the book were perhaps
less accurate than the later ones.

The first victim had reminded him of a certain Horace
Acres, who—he wrote—was to him the image of all that is
ugly and evil and despicable in this world. The second reminded him of someone not quite so evil as the first. The
third was not quite so evil as the second. And so on. By the
tenth, they reminded him of people whom he considered as
neither good nor bad. By the fifteenth, they had commenced
to remind him of friends. By the eighteenth, he saw a re-
semblance to one of his brothers, Wesley; actually the
brother he loved best.

After the tenth execution he began to have interviews with
those appointed to die, and he recorded to the best of his
ability the exact conversations. These interviews usually took
place immediately after he had installed the portable chair.
In the small towns he was allowed to visit with the prisoner

as long as he liked; in the larger towns the jailer was sometimes rather gruff and laconic and a stickler for the rules.
But every jailer, old or young, in large towns or small ones,
stood somewhat in awe of the executioner. Not once had
William Morgan failed to get his interview.

It was his habit to talk with the condemned for a while,
on the friendliest of terms, like a minister perhaps, and then
to ask quietly, "Do you know who I am?"

Not one had ever guessed. Which pleased him no end,
and satisfied many doubts that had roiled his mind in late
years. Not one had recognized him! And each, from the
eleventh to the nineteenth, had flushed deep red when he
announced, "I'm the State executioner. May God have tender
mercy on your soul." He had added the *tender* himself; a
work of art, he thought.

When he first reached Cross City, he found his assistant
already there going about the usual routine. He spoke
briefly to the jailer concerning the prisoner. That morning,
before leaving home, he had scribbled the following onto
the back of the registered letter sent to him from the State
capitol: *Maxwell (none) Harper, twenty-three years old,
veteran of North Africa, Italy, and Southern France; condemned to die for murder of Vance Acroft; time: four a. m.,
fourteenth of March.*

All the information he had scribbled on the back of the
letter, except the veteran bit, was carried in the letter itself,
which was more an official form than a letter. But it seemed

to him he might forget, and if he set the facts down in his own handwriting he might remember better.

From the newspaper stories he knew many other facts; from his father-in-law he knew that a reprieve was being sought. There was not much chance for a reprieve, he thought, and it was just as well. He imagined that such a delay was mere agony for the condemned; and besides, it was certainly a terrible inconvenience for the executioner.

Installing the chair was not difficult, and yet the work went extremely slow. Morgan paced about, telling his assistant, "Let's rush it up. Let's rush it up."

"What's your big hurry?" the assistant asked. It was only his third case and he was still nervous and jumpy. Besides, he was not a very good electrician, but rather, a good friend to a certain sheriff who had supported the Governor.

"I'm not in a hurry," Morgan said. "I'm hungry."

"Go eat something then," the assistant said. "You're not helping me much."

Morgan went to eat. When he returned, the chair was ready for his inspection. But he decided to delay the inspection until after the interview. The jailer was agreeable and actually unaware of the rules. It was his jail, so to speak, for he had paid for it: one-third of his salary went to the county sheriff, who had the power to appoint and fire him. He made his own rules, because—as he put it—he could tell in a flash who would do and who wouldn't.

They went upstairs and all the way back along a narrow

passage to the death cell, which was like the other cells, except for the small corridor with its second door, providing a space for visitors. There was plenty of light in the corridor. The jailer opened the first door and then asked if the executioner wished the second door opened.

"No! No!" Morgan said, as if the man who sat in the cell with his back to them were some kind of man-eating beast.

"Anyways," the jailer said, "I was jist gonna say I couldn't open the second door. 'Gin the law." The jailer left the two alone.

The prisoner sat with his arms on a wide plank which served as a desk. He was writing something. He had not moved at the sound of steps or the voices. Morgan watched him for almost a minute, and just as he was about to speak, the prisoner turned. Morgan drew a deep breath. He was by no means prepared for the tremendous impact caused by the face of the prisoner. Later, at home, he was unable to recall the color of the eyes or the shape of the mouth, or any of the details of the face. The intense quality of peacefulness was like nothing he had ever witnessed before. He actually trembled and lowered himself to the small bench beside the door.

"Do you want me?" the prisoner asked.

"No, I don't want you," Morgan answered. His voice spread without quality, for suddenly the idea had come to him that he was the condemned and the prisoner was the executioner. "Only to talk a minute," he added.

The prisoner moved to the corner of the bunk, which was no more than three or four feet from the door.

"Is there any hope?" Morgan whispered.

"For what?"

"For you."

The prisoner did not answer.

Morgan thought he saw the faint beginning of a smile. He was still uneasy and afraid. "I meant hope *here*—for a reprieve maybe."

"No. Why should there be?"

"But people are working for you. I happen to know they are."

"It's no use."

"To work?"

"No use to . . . to hope."

"Then you don't believe in hope?"

"Oh, I believe in it. But it's dangerous."

"Religion is based on hope, you know."

"Mine isn't."

"What then? Love?"

"Oh, maybe," the prisoner said wearily.

"Yes, yes," the executioner said excitedly. "You can say that because you are going to die. But what about the rest of us?"

"The rest? You're like all the others," the prisoner said. "You believe you're going to live forever."

"No! No, I don't believe that!" the executioner said.

"Yes, you do."

"Then you believe it too!"

The prisoner dropped his head. "I suppose so."

"Do you . . . do you believe you deserve to die?"

"I'm trying to decide."

"By writing it down?"

"Yes. Everything. All that happened, from the beginning."

The executioner was deeply moved. "Except, of course, there is no beginning to anything." After a moment he added, "If you die, I hope the next world will treat you better."

"I'm not a gambler," the prisoner said.

Morgan got up. The face of the prisoner was shaking him to pieces. He could feel an actual rattle about his heart, and again it seemed to him that he was the victim and the prisoner was the executioner. Also, the age of the prisoner worried him. He did not look older than twenty-three, but it seemed to Morgan that he should be much older. "How old are you?"

"Twenty-three."

"It's a great pity . . . that you're so young."

"Maybe not. If I were older . . . there would be more to kill."

"More? Of what?"

"I don't know. I was just talking. How do I know what I might become?"

"Yes! Exactly! That's what I've been thinking . . . for a long time. Exactly!" He grabbed one of the door bars for support. He was ready for his final and principal question. "Do you know who I am?"

"I think so."

"Who?"

"You are the executioner."

"You . . ." He was out of breath. "You are . . . the first . . . ever to guess it."

"I didn't guess," the prisoner said.

Morgan saw a smile, an absolute smile. A terrible, beautiful thing, like a jagged segment of lightning. He drew himself together and said quietly, with dignity, "May God have tender mercy on your soul." He clung to the bar. He was unable to let go.

The prisoner rose. "Thank you," he said. "When your time comes, may He also have tender mercy on you."

Morgan saw the words, he thought: a jagged streak, like the smile, a terrible and beautiful thing. He turned and fled down the narrow passage. He was unable to speak.

He drove home looking into the sun. With every heartbeat there was an explosion in his head that shook him from scalp to toes.

His wife was not alarmed by his headache, nor by his mood, nor by the fact that he had gone to bed so early. Her first concern commenced when she went upstairs to go to bed herself. She found him lying very still, staring toward the south window.

"Do you have to go back tomorrow, or did you finish?" she asked.

"I finished. Everything is ready."

"At four o'clock, isn't it?"

"Yes. Four o'clock."

"Why must it always be at such an odd hour?"

"I suppose there's a reason."

"Of course there's a reason, but what *is* it?" Before he could answer she added, "You're not worrying, are you?"

"No."

"Oh, yes you are."

"Then why did you ask me?"

"I wanted to know why . . . what worries you."

He got up and sat on the side of the bed. "The man. The way he looks. His actions. His voice."

"What *does* he look like?"

"To me . . . well . . . to me, he looks like Wesley."

"How ridiculous! Why, it's silly to think such a thing, much less to say it. Here!" She was out of bed so quickly that it startled him. From the hall outside their door she took a cane-framed picture of Wesley, brought it inside and held it before him. "Can you sensibly and honestly say that man looks like this?"

"No. No. He doesn't look like that at all."

"All right then!" She thought she had settled the matter forever.

"But I don't think Wesley looks like that either."

"Then what does he look like? Like the prisoner, I suppose?"

"'Yes. Exactly.'"

"Ah, now we're getting somewhere. He looks like Wesley, so Wesley looks like him. What is the matter with you? Of all the cases you've had . . . and this one, remember, was in cold blood. He killed a good man."

"How good?"

"I don't know that he was good. Maybe I meant harmless, innocent."

"How innocent?"

"Don't be infantile. Do you want me to say twenty pounds of something or twenty tons or three miles? What measurement do you want? He was a member of the church. . . ."

"Yes, I know that . . . but it doesn't answer anything."

"Answer, my foot. I'm sleepy and you ought to be."

"If you're sleepy, the best thing for you is to get some sleep."

"You're quite mad," she said.

"Very likely," he answered. "Very likely you are quite right."

Within a few minutes she was asleep.

Half an hour before midnight he got up, unnoticed, and went downstairs. At the desk in the living room he wrote two notes on the last page of his black book. The first was to his wife: "My dearest, I am sorry for this. If things had been different I would be different. But I am truly sorry for this."

The second note was addressed to "To Whom It May Concern." The paragraph was neat and unhurried: "He does not deserve to die. I know. I am tired. I have been tired as long as I can remember, but I know this clearly: there is always something the courts cannot find out. I will never be blamed for it. Whatever his secret is, I know it would save him. May God have tender mercy upon my soul."

The clock in the living room had not yet struck midnight when he placed the slender barrel of the revolver between his teeth and executed himself.

Early in the morning, when the world seemed dead except for a few pigeons and a few newsboys, a barber climbed the steps of the jail in Cross City. It was his duty to shave the head of the prisoner. He hurried, not because he liked the job before him, but because hurry was born in his bones and he had to do all things quickly. He was an Italian, a prisoner of war, brought to the camp near Cross City when North Africa fell to the Allies. After the war he had managed to remain in the area.

The barber wished to be as pleasant as possible, for that was his nature, and when he had clipped off a few handfuls of hair he spoke his first words to the prisoner. "You were among the war, no?"

The prisoner nodded. He held in his lap his manuscript, and as pieces of hair fell on it he blew the hair away. Now and then the barber glanced toward a special deputy, fully armed, standing outside the cell door.

"Is no good," the barber said.

"What?" the prisoner asked.

"Head without the hair is no good. Is ugly."

The prisoner blew the pieces of hair from his manuscript.

The barber worked with great concern. "Very excellent hair . . . very excellent."

The barber finished, and remained for a moment beside the prisoner. He wished there was something else he could do, something to make the head appear less vulnerable. He glanced back at the deputy, and bending over he whispered, "Maybe they cannot find someone to pull the switch. The executioner have kill himself. Holy Mother of God . . ."

He made the sign of the cross and went out.

The prisoner blew the remaining pieces of hair from his manuscript and began to read, as if the words were unfamiliar to him.

Part One

I

IT SNOWED the day we moved to Mister Sid Acroft's place, and the wagon ruts we left behind us were ours, alone, as if we owned the road and the whole world. We had moved once a year for every year that I could remember, but when we turned off the road, and cut across the pasture to the house, I had the feeling we would be there a long time. In many places the snow did not hide the raw red gullies, which lay like fresh wounds. But some were hidden, and Papa bounced across them, beating the mules and cursing, paying no attention to the sound of shattering glass.

"It's no need to act a fool," Mama said, but it was hardly a complaint. The next breath she was saying, "It's going to be a hard winter, mark my words. I feel sorry for them old folks." She was looking at the hill to our left where the Poor Farm was. It was not a farm, but merely a few acres with an old two-story house that seemed to be crowded between two chimneys. Smoke from the north chimney drifted down over a wide veranda full of empty rockers.

It was cold. I had wrapped a quilt around my shoulders and pushed my feet under the edge of a mattress; Rudy had crawled inside the roll of linoleum, leaving only his head outside. From time to time Mama would put her hand over his forehead to see if his fever was down, and when she would touch his head he would draw it inside the roll of rug, quick, like a turtle. It was a game they played, and it kept him from complaining about the sores on his legs when the jolting was bad.

The house was old, with three rooms and a hall. From a long way off we could hear the tin roof rattle in the wind. We could see, too, that the doors were standing open, as if the other tenants had left owing Mister Sid a good bit.

Papa backed the wagon to the kitchen door and we got out to push, for the ground around the doorsteps was soft from much dishwater and waste and the backing was diffi-cult. It was almost dark when the unloading was finished. I stood by the empty wagon holding my hand which I had mashed numb when the stove leg caught against the door jamb. From the slight cut the blood dripped down my fingers and into the snow. I looked at the spot between my feet, which was not red at all but an ugly purple.

"Don't stand there moping," Papa said, as if his hand had been mashed instead of mine.

I moved when he spoke and shook my hand to bring back the feeling. I knew he had remembered the axe. All that past year we had used Mr. Leatherman's axe, and I guess we would have brought it with us if Mr. Leatherman hadn't come early that morning, while we were loading, to take it away.

"We've got to git up some wood," Papa said.

"The axe . . ." I began, and looked about the barren yard as if I expected to find one.

"Well, don't stand there," Papa said. "Take the mules home and tell Mr. Acroft you want to borrow his axe."

I moved quickly, from habit, and in so doing my crippled foot slipped off the doubletree.

Papa cursed and said, "You're going to break your neck."

But I quickly recovered and was inside the wagon bed driving off before he could say anything more. I looked back at the wagon ruts in the snow and at the man standing near the kitchen door and I was glad when I was past the copse of pines where I could not see him. Rather, where he could not see me. Then I looked down at my foot and the tears came into my eyes, but not because my left foot was turned inside, exactly perpendicular to my right foot. My eyes watered because it was cold, and my ankle was skinned and my hand was mashed; because Rudy lay wrapped up in a quilt beside a cold hearth, for the beds were not yet up; because we had no axe; and because I was almost fifteen and did not care whether my eyes were wet or dry.

I drove the mules into the lot and stopped near the wagon shed and called to a boy whose name I wish I had never heard, whose face I wish I had never seen. He emptied a basket of corn over the fence onto the backs of a dozen hogs. Then he came toward me.

"Where's Mister Acroft?" I said.

"I'm Mister Acroft," he said. "Heir apparent to the throne." His eyes danced and the wind blew harmlessly across his curly black hair. He walked with power and cunning, and was proud of his fifteen years. But I am looking back now. Then, I did not even understand what he had said. But the years have taught me some tricks too and I understand what "heir apparent" means. More. I know where it came from. But he knew at fifteen and I knew years later, which makes a difference. I have sometimes thought one sentence might have changed my life. Suppose I had known to say back to him, "Go hang yourself by your heir apparent garters." If I had known to say that, we might somehow have been friends; at least, we might not have been enemies.

I said, "Where do you want the mules put?"

"Where do you think? In the hog pen?"

I climbed out of the wagon bed onto the doubletree. He stood and stared at my crippled foot. Then the goodness in him came to the surface momentarily and he stepped up to the mules and began to unhitch them.

"Don't you want the wagon put under the shed?" I asked.

"It doesn't matter," he said. He began to unhitch the lead mule. "You water them?"

"No."

"The pond's right down there."

I went, while he sat on the wagon tongue and watched me. It is all right to sit and watch, but not on a wagon tongue. Sitting on a wagon tongue is like swinging on a gate. But he was showing me a thing or two. When I returned he pointed to the gear shed and then to the stable where the mules belonged. He unlocked the crib, said, "Twelve ears apiece," and stood by the door and watched until the corn was in the troughs. Then he pointed to the loft and said, "Two blocks of hay."

"Apiece?"

"Apiece," he answered. "You're not feeding a pair of goats. We got that team in Memphis. I went with Papa."

Then I showed my weakness. I should have kept quiet, but I said, "I guess it's the best pair of mules I ever drove."

"You never drove much. We got another pair cost twice as much."

I started up the ladder, which wasn't a ladder at all but cracks in the wall, so that my left foot was no help in the climbing. I felt ashamed that he watched me and I was all the more clumsy because of it. He said nothing, only watched. When the blocks of hay were in the stable and I had chained the door, he said, "Did you tear it up?"

"No."

"Well, tear it up."

I opened the door and carefully pulled the blocks of hay apart. "Is there anything else?" I asked.

"I don't know. Is there?"

"We want to borrow your axe," I said.

"Haven't you got an axe?"

"Yes," I lied, "but I guess we lost it moving."

"I bet you'd lose your head if you didn't have it glued on your shoulders."

I had the good sense not to answer him and for a second he was defeated. "Aw, come on, we got lots of axes."

We did not go to the woodpile at the back of the house, and I was disappointed. Why I should have felt such an urge at that time to go near his house I do not know. But I remember that I thought he knew what I wanted and was seeing I did not get it. He picked up an axe from the tool shed and put it down for a better one. With his thumb he felt the blade and tested its sharpness. Quite agreeably he handed the axe to me and said, "That's a good one. You need a saw too?"

I noticed three or four cross-cut Simonds saws hanging on the racks. "Just an axe," I said.

"Watch it and don't cut your foot. It's sharp as hell."

As I turned the corner of the barn I heard him say, "Don't hurry."

"What?" I said.

"It's just a saying," he said, and in the dusk I thought I could read his amusement over confusing me.

I stood, making no move to go and he said, "The boss said you all were going to cook for the Poor House."

"Mama is," I said.

"Well, don't put no arsenic in Mr. ten Hoor's soup."

I noticed that I was shaking from the cold and my hand was throbbing again. I remembered I had been gone too long, so I turned and ran. When I was free of the lot and into the field road, a voice caused me to look back. Through the darkness I saw Mr. Acroft riding up to the lot gate on the most beautiful white horse I had ever seen. "Vance!" the voice called again.

"Yessir!"

Vance started quickly for the gate. I stood with some pleasure and watched him open and close the gate, while the big man rode through on his white charger like a knight, and came to a sudden halt. "Who left that wagon out?"

"He did."

"He who?"

"I don't know their names."

"Why didn't you put it up?"

"He was already unhitched. I didn't want to tell him to hitch up again."

"See if you can hitch up and put it under the shed where it ought to be."

"Yessir."

A sadness took hold of me, and I walked along slowly, stumbling sometimes in the dark, not even afraid of what Papa would say. I had started out that morning with a kind of new hope, the same feeling that a farmer will have when the earth grows warm in April; but now it was gone and I could feel the darkness moving toward me from every angle. Even so, if I could have known what was ahead of me, I might have dropped the axe in the creek and gone running away from Rudy, who was the one I loved most, in search of something better before it was too late. But little mercies have a way of coming along at the right time. I remember Papa took the axe without a word and we soon had a fire roaring in the stove and in the fireplace. The morning feeling, journey-hope, came back to me and I believed something good was waiting for us just around the corner of the week or the month.

We ate hot buttered cornbread and molasses and basked in the warmth, with not one scolding from Papa. Instead of going to bed in the iciness of the other room, we had a pallet before the fire, and we slept warm until way into the night.

2

FOR A while our life was calm and peaceful, and it seemed we had lived there forever as rightful and natural parts of the universe. Though when I think back, I know it was not a good time for Rudy. We got up at four o'clock in the morning. Just before six Papa would go off to Mr. Acroft's sawmill and Mama would go to the Poor House, which we called The House, to get breakfast for thirty-one old people, most of whom could not wipe their mouths properly after a meal. At seven I went off to school, which was only a mile away, and left Rudy alone. I have often wondered what those hours meant to him, what he did, what he thought. School was out of the question for him until his legs were better. The sores always came on him in the summer but by October they were usually gone. Only this year they had stayed, for we had picked cotton all fall in heavy dews and the spots which had been red and white turned brown and grew larger. "Just a little dew poisoning," Papa said, and his mind went on to other things.

"The first payday I git I'm gonna take you to a doctor, young man," Mama would say. And Rudy was both proud and afraid. "I'll tell you what," she would add, "we'll take Max along and let the doctor look at his foot. Why, Aunt Pardy was telling me about a boy had his foot put straight by this doctor. Only seventy-five dollars too . . ." Oh, she could say it well, as if seventy-five dollars wasn't much at all. We would sit by the fire and talk and it would seem easy and certain. But when Papa came in she wouldn't talk any more and the plan would die down with the fire, down, down to the last ember, but never completely gone. Just as the fire was never gone, for we covered it with ashes from night to morning and there was no need for matches.

Supper was early at The House. I would go and help Mama wash the dishes and walk home with her. I soon came to know all the people and I liked most of them. I remember how they built their little worlds, as if their feet walked the morning of their life instead of the sunset. Why I should say "little worlds" I do not know, for I have come to understand that any world is large and the universe stretches out equidistant in every direction.

My own was a world of feet. I walked with my head down, I stood with my head down, eternally watching the way others moved from one place to another. Maybe I hoped to find that one person whose foot was shaped like mine, who understood my world, whose heart could sing with mine behind the wall of loneliness in the land where every man must live at one time or another.

I remember how my heart leaped once when I thought I had found this thing in an old woman, sitting on the side of her bed, too old and too weak to make her way to the table for food. She had a room at the end of the hall next to Aunt Pardy's room, but I had never been inside nor seen her, though a few times I had heard her singing, low and far off, not for the world but for herself. One night I carried a tray of food to her and when I pushed back the door the raw glare of the light hanging over her dresser made me blink. She sat on the edge of her bed, facing me and the door, and the black right toe of her old oxfords pointed out from beneath her gown like a sword. The left shoe, almost covered, lay at right angles like another sword, angry, threatening, ready to plunge its way through a foot that sat so nice and straight. The tray shook in my hands.

"Are you afraid of me?" she asked.

"Nome, I'm not afraid."

"Why, honey, I'm Old General Carpenter's daughter, and I can tell you here and now I've no right to be in this place. I had my money put away in the bank. Not much, but enough to take care of an old woman. Banks this and banks that. Well, they walked off with it. They're thieves. Plain, ordinary, night-prowling thieves. And worse. Worse than a chicken thief, who at least is usually ragged and hungry. They walked off with it in their fine Sunday suits. Or worse, rode off in a brand-new automobile. Oh, their day's coming all right. They can't take my money and buy their way past St. Peter. Can they?"

"Nome."

"What are you staring at, child? Who are you anyway?"

"Mama . . . she sent this in to you."

"You . . . yes . . . Well, I'll eat it. I'm not hungry but we have to eat to live, don't we? Your mammy can cook, only they don't give her nothing to fix with but collards and corn meal. Do you know what I'd like to have? Some walnuts. You bring me a poke of walnuts and I'll tell you what I'll give you: I'll give you a quarter. If you don't believe I've got it, look here." Then she picked up her left shoe, which had not been on her foot at all, and poured out sixty cents into her lap. My face clouded with the sudden realization that her foot was not like mine.

"You're afraid I won't pay you?"

"Nome."

"I'll pay you now."

"Nome. I'll bring them if I can find any." I put the tray down beside her.

"Why, honey, the woods are full . . . unless the thieves took the walnuts off too." She made a little laugh and turned to her food.

I do not remember the first time I went into Mr. ten Hoor's room, but I knew from the beginning it was not like any other room in The House. It was a corner room on the first floor with a fireplace which I later learned had no chimney. The wide, tall mantel was covered with books and at either side of the hearth there were racks with magazines dating back ten or fifteen years. Near the window was an old iron bed, green brass, and across the foot rail a green afghan which was probably the oldest thing in the room. In one corner, away from the fireplace, was a washstand, a beautiful wash bowl and pitcher. On every wall, except the mantel wall, there was a group of bird pictures hung in triangles against the yellowed paper. Over the mantel was a picture of Jesus. There was a rocker, always by the hearth, and one straight chair, always at the foot of the bed, facing the window. A single, naked light hung from the center of the ceiling.

Mr. ten Hoor first spoke to me in the kitchen. It was supper time and I was helping because Mama had had a spell of coughing and was not feeling well. Mr. ten Hoor sat at the head of the table, erect, and thin, except for his hands which were swollen with arthritis. His eyes were clear, almost harsh, and the skin on his face was tight, drawn back, somewhat in the same way that his hair was slicked down. It was obvious that he was the leader of that group, for when he clasped his hands and lifted them toward his chin, the others eyed him and slowly dropped their heads. I was still bringing more plates, as no one knew ahead of time whether there would be fourteen or twenty-eight at the table for a meal. When his prayer was finished and the noise of silverware had begun, Mr. ten Hoor looked directly at me.

"Young man, did you bow your head?" he asked.

"Nossir."

"In the future, will you be kind enough to bow your head in the presence of words of grace?"

Somehow catching the rhythm of his words, I answered, "Yessir, I will be kind enough."

"Thank you." He nodded. "And I recommend closing the eyes." The noise of eating had momentarily stopped. "You may wonder," he went on, "why I suspected you if my own head was bowed and eyes closed. Well, sir, it was a premonition. A simple premonition. Nothing more. Mrs. Mullen, I thank you for the peas, please."

Mrs. Clements, who obviously admired the man at the head of the table, had the peas passed before Mrs. Mullen could touch the dish. "Do tell . . ." she said. "Mr. ten Hoor, you're out of this world."

"Madam," he answered, "we're all destined to be out of this world shortly. I hope we face that realization with persistent equanimity."

"Faith!" Mrs. Lock shouted. "And Amen to you, Brother ten Hoor. The Lord never sent nobody more troubles than he could bear."

"Maybe so," Mrs. Clements said, "but I couldn't bear to lose Mr. ten Hoor. Had you ever thought what this place would be like without him?"

"It would be, Mrs. Clements, exactly what you chose to make it. 'Stone walls do not a prison make, nor iron bars a cage. . . .' " Mr. ten Hoor sniffled with concern. "I must say, however, I shall miss every one of you when I cross over. Provided, of course, we are allowed the grand courtesy of remembering, on the other side of Jordan."

"Now you hush," Mrs. Mullen said. "You've got Aunt Pardy to crying."

"Equanimity, Aunt Pardy," Mrs. Clements said. "Remember the words of Mr. ten Hoor."

"Equa-stuff-and-nonsense," Aunt Pardy cried. "You all know I'm not afraid. You just leave me alone."

"Exactly," Mr. ten Hoor said. "Mrs. Mullen, would you be kind enough to pass the pepper sauce. I shouldn't, of course, but a mere drop could hardly be fatal, and it might greatly enhance the flavor of these peas."

"Enhance?" Mrs. Clements asked.

"Yes, enhance."

"What's the meaning of that word?"

"Mrs. Clements, you know it is against my policy to define words. I should be happy to lend you my dictionary, day or night."

"Does it start with an 'i'?" Mrs. Clements asked.

" 'A'," Mrs. Boatler said, "when I went to school."

"She is speaking of the word 'enhance,' " Mr. ten Hoor said. "It is initiated by the letter 'e'."

Mrs. Clements nodded. "Thank you, Mr. ten Hoor."

"Yours," he answered.

"There's times," Aunt Pardy said, drying her eyes and leaving bread crumbs on her cheeks, "when I just git the all-overs." And she went back to crying again.

It was some days later that I began to go regularly to Mr. ten Hoor's room. Most of his past remained a mystery to me, but from time to time fragments of information came to the surface. I learned he had once been a teacher in the local grammar school, and had had some kind of unfortunate experience with Vance Acroft. The following year, his contract was not renewed, and he moved on to another rural school, where, before the term was finished he became ill. He attributed his move, as well as his broken health, to the Acrofts. He continually laid his misfortune at their feet, and yet it was done with subtlety, for he was a master in drawing delicate distinctions. Whether my mind absorbed his warnings, his own mistrust, I do not know; whether my devotion to Mr. ten Hoor was a thorn in Vance's side, I do not know.

Again, who can say what is chance and what is answer? In the end, it was more than one thing that brought me to my knees. Small comfort to be sure, but it is the small comforts that feed us daily, for the great ones come only after the small ones have been swept away and hunger has set in.

I know I should be just in weighing these matters, but who can be just? A man's mind is the scales and his heart is the balance, and the weight of a matter depends on the heaviness of the heart. So perhaps I blame Mr. ten Hoor. But that is wrong. I am unjust. Maybe tomorrow I will find no blame in my heart to place against him.

"Can you read well?" he asked me. His room was cold and the naked light hung down like the last fading spark of heat on this earth.

"I can read," I said.

With some effort he crawled into his bed and pulled the green afghan about his shoulders. "I'm old," he said, "and my heart has better vision than my eyes. Read to me."

"What from?" I asked. "The Bible?"

"Not tonight. Tonight I feel no kinship with the Prophets and only the slightest sympathy for St. Paul. Dickens will do."

"Don't you go to church?" I asked.

"Church? My boy, the Church wore out my soul. I am a believer in Jesus. What more could a man ask of me? Church is for those who do evil and have need of expiation. For the politicians, let us say, who sell their souls for money.

I might sell my soul—a part of it anyway—for a book, only for a book."

"If you sold your soul for enough money," I said, "you could buy all the books you want."

"Dickens," he said, sternly, "there it is on the end of the mantel."

"You never answered me," I said.

"What is chance and what is an answer? Why, we're killing time, boy. I may answer you tomorrow or the next day or next year. The words that come out of me are chance and the sum of seventy years of living and if you were wise you would listen. I said I may answer you tomorrow."

"Tomorrow, I may not come," I said.

"Of course you will come tomorrow."

"How do you know?"

"I know because there is no other beauty in your life; I know because I like you; I know because I have vision."

"Why do you like me? I've never done anything for you."

"I like you because you are both old and young. It is the most beautiful combination on earth. You are quite beautiful."

"I am not!" I said.

"Very well, you are not. You are an old man with beautiful feet."

"You leave me alone!" I cried.

"Dickens," he said. "It is there on the end of the mantel."

I crossed the room. I was shaking. I held the book with

some difficulty and stood while I read. At last he interrupted me.

"You must not tell Vance about this reading."

"Why?"

"Because he will be bitter and angry with you."

"He's already bitter and angry with me."

"Very well. Tell him anything you like. Tell him we get along famously together. Alas, poor Yorick, I know him well. He was once my favorite."

"Vance was?"

"Quite. A very dark angel with a very bright mind. A fallen angel who wishes others to fall. Don't cross swords with him."

"I'm not afraid of him."

"I speak of his mind, not his fists. Let us forget the matter and go to *the Dickens.* Ha! ha! ha!"

His laughter upset me. I began to read again. And the light over my shoulder was like the last fading spark of heat on this earth.

3

FEBRUARY was a terrible month. It began with Papa getting drunk, an unmerciful spree which had endless consequences. At the same time, in spite of Mr. ten Hoor's warning, I unwittingly crossed swords with the fallen angel, and for the first time tasted a bit of my own downfall.

Mr. Emmett, who was the sawyer at the sawmill, came to our house for supper one Saturday. He sat at the head of the table, after Papa's insistence, talking and shining and showing a great deal of warmth for Papa, who had shared Mr. Emmett's fruit jar of liquor. Papa was quite agreeable too and more than once he showed concern for the condition of Rudy's legs, which were much better, for Mama had had a payday and she had taken him to the doctor as was promised.

"He needs iron," Papa explained, and Rudy would smile and shift from one foot to the other as he stood beside the stove, for there were not enough chairs for him to sit at the table. He was so thin and his hair was so white that he looked like a little old man.

"Show him your medicine," Papa said.

Rudy ran to the cook table and brought the bottle, which Papa uncorked and held to Mr. Emmett's nose.

"Iron," Papa said.

Mr. Emmett sniffed and frowned and said, "Iron all right."

"What they can't do . . ." Papa said. "What the doctors can't do . . ."

Mr. Emmett interrupted to say, "My daddy had a uncle who was a doctor. Perkins. Hardy Perkins. He got rich and died. . . ."

"What they can't do," Papa insisted, "just ain't hardly thought up." He pointed at me. "Why, they can straighten that boy's foot for seventy-five dollars."

"Aw," Mr. Emmett said.

"That's right," Papa said.

"When?" Mr. Emmett asked.

"Well . . ." Papa said. "If the Lord's willing and I keep my health . . ."

"Sawmilling's dangerous," Mr. Emmett said.

"It shore God is," Papa said. "I'll be glad when crop time comes."

"Over in Tedga County a few year back," Mr. Emmett said, "I was cuttin' some hickory crossties and if anything will pull the guts out of a engine that will and the belt split and drug this feller I mean slap dab through the saw. He left a wife and a houseful of kids. I'll tell you who she was. She was a Malone and her daddy broke hisself running for sheriff. Got beat once by sixty votes and another time by eighty-some-odds. He finally moved to Texas."

"I never been to Texas," Papa said.

"Big, my Lord, it's big," Mr. Emmett said, and noticing Mama he said, "Excuse me, Miss Audie."

"That's all right," Mama said. She was paying no attention to him anyway. It was late and she was tired, after three meals of cooking and washing at The House.

"This boy is smart," Papa said, pointing to me again. "Spell something for Mr. Emmett."

"Spell *asafetida*," Mr. Emmett said.

"I can't," I answered.

"I can't neither," Mr. Emmett said.

"He can spell it," Papa said. "He's just scared."

"We've got to go," Mr. Emmett said, and got up. "Mighty fine meal, Miss Audie."

"It's not much," Mama said. And it wasn't.

They went off together, warm friends. The red in Papa's face, which always began in his forehead, had moved down to his cheeks. But we knew he would be all right until it reached his chin and started moving down his throat.

Papa did not come home that night. Early in the morning, before Rudy and I were awake, Mama got up and built a fire and went to The House. When I awoke I could hear somebody calling from the pine thicket just below our house. I could hear the fire crackling in the other room and could see the narrow strips of light coming through the walls and the make-shift door and window. "You say it once more and I'll kill you!" the voice cried.

"Blue belly!" another voice said, which belonged to Papa.

In a few minutes somebody shook the front door, and before I could get as far as the fireplace, there was a lunge and the door latch splintered to pieces. Papa went past me and into the kitchen where the shotgun hung over the flour barrel. When he came back into the room, Rudy was standing beside me, trembling, holding my hand. Papa looked at us and said, "Why didn't you open the door? You want me to git shot?"

"I . . . I was . . ." Then a cry came from the pine thicket again.

"Just hush," Papa said. He started out the front door, turned, and went out the kitchen door. He crouched behind the well box and called, "You're a lousy Blue belly, Charlie Emmett, and I ain't afraid of your owl-head neither."

After a few seconds, we saw him crawl along the ground a few feet, gain a gulley, and run for another thicket of trees a hundred yards below the pines.

"Would it kill you if a bullet was to come through this house?" Rudy asked.

"I don't know," I said.

"I bet it would if it come through a crack," Rudy said. "What's a owl-head?"

"A pistol."

"You rather have a pistol or a shotgun?"

"I don't know," I said. "Be quiet."

"You better go tell Mama," he said.

"Why?"

"Because Papa's going to git killed."

"I can't help it."

"You wouldn't care, would you?"

"No."

"I would," Rudy said.

"I don't care if you care."

"I'd care because we'd have to go to the funeral. You ever been to a funeral, Buddy?"

"Yes."

"I never been. But I know what it's like."

"You've been," I said.

"When?"

"To grandma's."

"I don't remember it."

"You went, just the same."

"I won't have to go to Papa's funeral because I ain't got nothing but overalls and you can't wear overalls to a funeral, can you?"

"I guess you could."

"I bet you if Papa was to git killed Mr. Acroft would buy me a pair of pants to wear. I bet you he would. You reckon he would?"

"I don't know."

"Mama could cut the legs off of that pair you got from Azel. Only, I guess they'd still be too big. And I'm not going in my overalls!" Rudy cried.

"He ain't dead yet," I said. "And I wish you'd hush. We couldn't hear a shot if it was fired."

We stood by the kitchen door waiting until we got tired. Then we went back into the living room and sat on the floor in front of the hearth, wanting to play bump-jacks, but we were afraid we might get shot if we went into the yard for rocks. The fire died down and we got so hungry I took a skillet and cooked us all the eggs I could find.

"I sure wish we had some bump-jacks," Rudy said.

I stretched out on the floor and went to sleep.

Rudy woke me up. "I'll go git the rocks," he said. "I ought to go anyway."

"I don't reckon you ought to go no more than me," I said.

"It ought to be me," he said, "because if I was to git killed you'd have some pants to wear, but if you was to git killed I wouldn't have nothing but overalls."

I tried to go back to sleep.

"And besides," Rudy said, "I'd rather git killed anyway than for you to."

So I got up and took the hammer and chipped off some pieces of rock from the chimney. They didn't make very good bump-jacks but we managed to play until the fire was completely gone and we heard two shots, one right after the other, in the woods. We jumped up and ran to the kitchen door and peeped out. After a while, Papa yelled, "Blue belly!"

"I'll kill you!" the other voice cried.

The woods stayed quiet and we finally went back to the hearth.

"What's a Blue belly?" Rudy asked.

"It's a Yankee."

"Mr. Emmett's not a Yankee. He's like everybody else."

"I can't help what he's like," I said. "He comes from up in Kentucky where it snows."

"It snows here," Rudy said.

"I'm tired explaining," I said.

"Well, I'm tired waiting," Rudy said.

It was past noon. The wood was gone and only a nest of dead coals lay in the ashes. Then Mama came home, cold and tired, and before we could explain, she flew into us about the fire. Rudy told her how it was. She picked up the door-latch pieces and put them on the coals and I went out for wood before she told me to. Rudy kept on explaining. "He was red down to here." He touched the hollow of his throat. "Wasn't he, Max?"

"No," I said, and touched my Adam's apple. "Only to here, just past his goozle."

Then it seemed like Mama got afraid. She took my arm and shook me. "You go over to Mr. Acroft's and you tell him to come over here and stop them two! You hear?"

I started out. "What if Mr. Acroft's not at home?"

"You wait on him. Lord! Lord! If it's not one thing, it's two. Looks like I wasn't meant to have a minute's peace. I just wish I'd never brought you younguns into this world."

I went out.

"Stay away from them woods," Mama called.

"Don't worry," I said.

I followed the field road until I came to the gate, and all the way I was thinking how hard it would be to carry out my mission, for Vance would certainly be there, his eyes grinning and demanding, "So you want the Boss to come save your pappy? What for?"

What for? That's what I wanted to know too. I am not saying I did right, but I did stop at the gate and consider for a long time. Would Mr. Acroft go and if he went, what if he got shot? But the answer hinged on Vance. I did not want him to laugh at me. When he came into the yard a few minutes later, I hid behind the crib.

From the corner of the crib, I saw Vance running beside the fence, and his sister ran behind him with a scarf flying about her head. She called him mean names and I knew he had done some devilish thing to her. But I was concerned only for myself: I wished not to be seen. At the right moment I ran from the crib into the alley of the barn. The barn was full of stock, so I picked a stable where a few calves stood nibbling the trampled hay and hid under the manger. For a long time I could hear the chase outside and the name calling, and I tried to think about how Margo looked. She was a year older than Vance and she had a round face and big gray eyes and long hair that shone like polished oak. Yet, they favored, especially across the nose and mouth. Two or three times she had spoken to me, at a distance, and I knew right away she was not as smart as Vance. When they came running through the alley I wanted to raise up and look, but I was afraid I might be caught.

I think I went to sleep. I know it was warm there and the

time passed off well. While I waited I heard three shots and I tried to make out which was pistol and which was shotgun. The only thing that worried me was the lie I would have to tell Mama: I would have to say Mr. Acroft was not at home. Then, when that was heaviest on my mind, I heard Margo and Vance again, and she said, "Papa will tend to you when he gets home." All was well. I leaned my head on the sill and if I did not go to sleep, at least the time slipped by without my knowledge and it was suddenly dusk. I got up and ran home.

"You took your own precious time," Mama said.

"Mr. Acroft wasn't at home," I said.

All three of us went to The House, which was like a cage of growling, hungry old animals, because supper was very late and what we had was hardly enough to be missed.

Mr. ten Hoor, who was also fretted and hungry, sat at the head of the table and prayed, "Almighty, help us to cease this bickering and cleanse our hearts and souls so that this scant nourishment will be sufficient to sustain us in our humble efforts to do Thy will. And Amen."

"And Amen," Mrs. Clements said. "Mr. ten Hoor, your words have fed me. I feel better already."

"Splendid. I'm always happy to learn that my words have served as a few spiritual crumbs."

"Not crumbs," Mrs. Clements said, "not crumbs at all."

"Thank you, madam. Would you be kind enough to pass

the collards. They create a tiny flame inside me, but a pinch of soda will quench . . ."

"Careful, Mr. ten Hoor. You know very well soda can put you out like a light."

"True. But I can think of no more beautiful way of passing from this terrestrial sphere: out like a light. Instantaneous fusion with the element of darkness. How simple, how beautiful! In that case, I might become a black cloud."

"Horrible! Horrible!" Mrs. Mullen shrieked. "You might come back mewing and scratching at my door."

"I beg your pardon, madam. I said black *cloud*. I have no communion with cats and merely the barest sympathy. Their claws annoy me, and their attitude is obsequious."

"Besides," Mrs. Clements said, "they don't have wings, and I'd bet my seat at this table for a solid week that Mr. ten Hoor gits a pair of wings when he crosses over Jordan."

"Jordan . . ." Aunt Pardy said. "Jordan . . ."

"Better hush," Mrs. Mullen said. "We'll have Aunt Pardy at it again."

"Let him go on," Mrs. Clements said. "Mr. ten Hoor, you talk good enough to run for Governor."

"No, madam. I ran for Justice-of-the-Peace once and endured an *overwhelming* setback. A veritable sausage of a man defeated me."

"No!"

"Yes, Mrs. Clements, 938 votes to 163."

"There!" Aunt Pardy said. "If that ain't overwhelming, what would you call it?"

"Precisely!" Mr. ten Hoor said. "You may understand how I've come to look on politics with a jaundiced eye."

"Ah," Mrs. Lock groaned. "You've lost faith!"

"No, Mrs. Lock. On the contrary, I have the utmost faith in the machinery of democracy. But the engineers often arouse my suspicions." He paused for a moment. "Nevertheless, I am too old to cry rebellion on the Public Square, and too tired to take my lantern and search for an honest man. What, I ask you, if I should find him? What then? Make him dishonest? No, let him go his way and I'll go mine, and whatever peace and happiness I encounter, I shall pray for the wisdom to understand and accept it. Ah, I am too old and the oil runs too low in my lantern. The Lord promised us three score and ten, and I've already been blessed with a few months beyond that. Mrs. Harper, the bread is good."

Mama nodded, a cool, half-hearted nod, for she did not care what Mr. ten Hoor thought of her bread making.

"In my opinion," Mrs. Lock said, "there is nothing like good cornbread and thick, sour buttermilk."

"In my opinion," Mr. ten Hoor said, "a loaf of bread and a jug of wine is superior."

"Do tell," Mrs. Clements said. "You're not a drinker?"

"Not exactly. I have, however, occasionally looked upon the liquid when it was red. That was quite some time ago, before the Baptists joined up with the bootleggers to drive the wicked serpent out of the garden."

Mr. Porter, who had never said a word in my presence, dropped his fork and shook his finger. "I say it ain't right to drive hit out of this here state to somebody else's back door. We ought to be willin' to tote our own share of sin and not shove hit off on somebody else!"

"Splendid!" Mr. ten Hoor said. "A splendid angle of judgment."

Mr. Porter nodded and shook and scraped his fork all over his plate in search of food.

"Well," Mrs. Porter said. "Nelse shore never shoved none off on nobody else."

"It's the Sabbath," Aunt Pardy said. "No argumints."

"Might as well be argumints as shootin'," Mrs. Porter said. "And I heered shootin' all day long."

Rudy and I looked at Mama, who was standing near the window as if listening for another shot. I went over and stood beside her with the back of my hand against hers. I wanted to catch her fingers and hold them, but that was something I had not done for years.

We cleared the table and washed the dishes, and while Mama was checking through The House I went to Mr. ten Hoor's room.

"So you came?" he said.

"Not for long."

He pulled the afghan from his shoulders. "Be precise. Are you refusing my offer of employment?"

"I don't know what you're talking about."

"I spoke to your mother this morning. Hasn't she spoken to you yet?"

"About what?"

"I offered you a job—with her permission."

"What kind of job?"

"She will explain."

"I think you're very strange," I said.

He squirmed with displeasure, caught himself, and fixed his eyes on me with authority. "I don't mind being strange, not so much anyway. But I detest the idea of being a stranger. We are not strangers, are we?"

"I don't know if we are or not."

"The sword of youth is cruel," he said. "It wounds without discretion."

"I don't know what you're talking about," I said.

"So much the better. The wound is already healing. The old are easily wounded, my son. They do not make good soldiers, for they know the battle is nearly over. If you find me tiresome . . . just, well, just tell me so."

"I came to see you."

"Ah, how right! How perfectly right and splendid. And I sit here babbling because I am afraid . . . afraid . . . afraid. You reach out to catch a butterfly, shining in the sunlight, and what happens? Either it eludes you, or else its

exquisite wings are crushed beneath the pressure of too much
eagerness. The good moments of life are like so many butter-
flies, and time leaves the fingers stiff and awkward. Read to
me. Dickens will do. When you read it warms my soul."

"I can't read tonight. I have to go."

"All right. Go to the washstand and look in the mirror."

"Why?"

"Because I have something to teach you."

I went and looked.

"Do you understand that you are handsome? Why do you
walk through this world with your head down? Why? Look
at me and answer."

I looked at him. "I think about things."

"Yes. Well, too much remembering is a sin. Is the foot
painful?"

"No."

"You must stop remembering it. Remember your face.
Make them look at your eyes. Your eyes have more power
than a hundred feet. It hurts my heart to see you hiding
them. Up. Up all the time. There. That's better. You may
go now."

"Good night," I said.

"God be with you."

"Sir?"

"God be with you."

"Yessir."

At home we found Papa lying in the kitchen door, groaning and jerking with cold. We dragged him to the fireplace and built a fire and left him beside the hearth. After a while he stopped groaning and shaking, and lay with his mouth open, breathing regularly.

"What did Mr. ten Hoor want with me?" I asked Mama.

"He wanted to hire you to stay with him at night and bring him water and carry his night chamber and read to him."

"I don't want to."

"He'll pay you a quarter."

"For how long?"

"Every night, he said."

"He's in the Poor House. Where would he get any money? If he had . . ."

"He said he'd pay you a quarter!" Her voice was sharp. "You could put it up. You could hide it, and pretty soon you'd have enough for your foot. . . ."

"I won't do it," I said.

"Don't tell me what you'll do and won't do! I've had enough trouble come my way today. Go to bed. Both of you."

When we were in bed, she came with one of Papa's jumpers, which she had warmed, and wrapped it about our feet.

Rudy lay close with his arm tight about me. "You won't go, will you, Buddy?"

"No."

"It's a lot of money. Mama might make you." After a while he said, "I wouldn't mind so much if it was summer. But I would still mind some."

"I'm not going to do it," I said.

"Why?"

"Because I don't reckon I like Mr. ten Hoor."

"If you don't like him, why do you go see him all the time?"

"I don't go see him all the time. Besides, I want to go to sleep. I'm tired."

"Well, I'm tired too and I'm sad."

"What about?"

"I'm just sad," he said.

It was the next day that I first saw the steps on the stairway which I was destined to climb. It seems now that I should have seen everything clearly, that I should have read, and having read, acted in the light of understanding. At least, I might have done something wiser than brand him a mortal enemy. I might have told Mr. ten Hoor what Vance had done. But wisdom does not arise with need, any more than one's feet become whole the moment one feels the urge to run. That day was the beginning of a terrible dream: I was both asleep and awake and therefore powerless. And yet it seems like nothing more than an ugly joke. An ugly childhood joke. As Mr. ten Hoor used to say: "Cry *why* until the echoes echo, and still there is no changing of the past, which is all I have and all you have too, because we do not understand the moment until it exists and once it exists it is gone from us."

He used to say lots of things about poets and time and death and life and how if one sparrow in all the unrecorded eons had lived one hour beyond its appointed time the constellations might have crashed. And I suppose, too, he said that wisdom does not arise with need. But lots of times I never paid any attention at all to what Mr. ten Hoor said.

It was a cold, threatening day. The clouds hung low in windblown patterns, and all that morning I looked out the window, thinking of a hundred things, of Rudy before the hearth, perhaps baking a sweet potato in the ashes. Papa had gone to work all right and so had Mama, and why the day should have hung so oppressively I do not know. A while before noon recess, Vance sent a note across the room to me which read: "Moo!" I crumpled it into my pocket, thinking he was merely picking at me because I was in the mulligrubs. I forgot the note and continued to think over the details of our lives. The road ahead seemed so long, so barren, so ugly that I dropped my face onto my desk in a gesture of hopelessness. I remained there when the others marched out for noon recess. Either the teacher did not notice me or she did not care to bother me, for she too went out without a word.

While the fit of depression was still upon me, I realized that people were entering the room. I did not look up though I knew I was being surrounded. I was too far down in the gray world of apathy.

"Moo!" a voice said.

I looked up into the face of Vance, who was sitting on the desk in front of me. His eyes were great orbs of light and shadow, full of little demons, busy as puppets. On either side of him, four or five others stood, almost lurking in the gray light of the room.

I hardly remember the names of those beside Vance, but there are times when their faces come to me as vividly as the shape of an oak leaf. They stood there in their clean overalls, for it was Monday and their clothes were not yet soiled; they were grinning and waiting for Vance, who was the undisputed leader. Even then, I think some faint wonder crossed my mind that these overalled, share-cropping, pellagra-faced five should let Vance lead them. But he led, and he owned them: all of them and the earth and starched khaki pants and silk-smooth jackets. They were on edge for him. He rapped on the desk with his fist and announced the court in session.

He spoke in a lofty manner, which evidently impressed his henchmen. "You, Max Harper, are hereby charged with a horrible crime, committed on the Sabbath Day, yesterday, between two and five o'clock, or thereabouts. How does the prisoner plead, Guilty or Not Guilty?"

I stared at them. No doubt it was a wild and confusing stare.

"Plead!" one of the overalled said, and he slapped me across the face with his rusty hand.

I kicked out the best I could and caught his shin with a glancing, not a solid, blow. A second pair of hands shoved me back into my seat, and a second slap struck me somewhere in the face. Vance had not moved, but all the overalls were closer now, and I could smell the odor of bodies. They were against me; they who ate what I ate, who wore the kind of clothes I wore.

"Answer the charge," Vance said.

"What charge?" I said.

"You are charged with unnatural association with animals."

"Now!" a voice to my left cried. "Guilty or Not Guilty."

"Calves!" another cried.

"Moo!" another added.

"You're a tookel!" Vance said. "A tookel! We now brand you with the Scarlet T!" They swarmed over me. I felt crayon burn on my forehead. Somehow I broke free and jumped up in my seat. I was wild and I was afraid. I lunged toward Vance, but he was too quick for me. "I'll kill you!" I cried. "I'll kill you if it's the last thing I do on this earth."

4

IT WAS some time before I had a chance to attempt to carry out my threat. In the meantime, hate lay coiled in me like a viper, continuously thrusting its forked tongue against my brain. This new burden seemed quite beyond my ability to bear. Vance and any of his cohorts had only to look at me and my face would flush with shame and humiliation and anger and hate. That, alone, was ample proof to them of my guilt.

An hour after the accusation, it seemed to me the whole world knew and believed. Every glance, every syllable directed toward me seemed to be charged with the horrible knowledge.

I could feel a fever rising in me. My cheeks grew warmer and warmer and my head and eyes ached with a dull pain which was so real it seemed to have an odor of its own. Ugly noises came from my stomach; the girls heard and sniggered and I wished fervently that I might die.

At last, when I could stand it no longer, I ran out of the classroom and around the corner of the building, where I began to vomit. Then the world grew dark and I sank slowly to my knees and fell back harmlessly against the house. The calmest, most peaceful wind I have ever felt blew across me. My mind was active enough that I thought I was dying. I was glad and not at all afraid. And this is strange: in that last split second of consciousness I saw the face of Vance; his smile was innocent and friendly and there were no demons in his eyes.

When I came to my senses, someone had my hand pulling me to my feet. About me was the noise of excited students but my ears heard only the ugly, thumping sound my crippled foot had made as I ran from the classroom. The teacher, who was kind but nerve worn, quickly made arrangements to send me home in the company of Vance and one of his henchmen. I ignored her plans and started off alone. Before I was out of earshot, somebody was telling the world at large how my granddaddy had died in the state asylum for lunatics. But that did not bother me then, perhaps because it was the truth.

That night I did not go to The House to help with the dishes and walk home with Mama. I brought in plenty of wood and water and then went to bed, attended faithfully by Rudy. From the miserable details of that day I am glad that I can recall at least one good thing: Rudy's concern for my well being. For one thing, he was lonely; but for a better thing, he was of the disposition to love unselfishly, and as much as anyone I have ever known he was able to feel deeply the hurt of others. Even then I wondered what someday he might become, but we were destined never to know the answer.

Mama and Papa arrived almost at the same time, both of them in an ugly mood. Rudy, in his efforts to attend me, had let the fire die down; and that caused the initial disturbance. My failure to appear at The House was another, and so on. Back of it all, of course, was the chaos of our lives. If we could have had some order in our lives, the days of gloom would have been merely a temporary shade separating us from the sunlight. But there was no order and therefore no kindness; and so I know there is no end to what the heart will endure. In that desolate and trying season we might have built with mere words something to warm us, just as we built a fire with our hands; but there was nothing, not even a laugh.

"What's the matter with you?" Mama asked.

I came from my room to the hearth and stood barefooted giving an account of myself, but revealing nothing. "I'm all right now," I said.

"You're no sicker than I am," she said. That was true and I was ashamed. Before I could answer, she was seized with a spell of coughing and it was fully five minutes of continuous choking and gasping, painful even to hear. At the end of it, Papa entered abruptly, pushing back the chair which held the latchless door.

"Why, what's the matter?" he asked, as if he had never heard her cough before.

"What do you think?" she asked, almost strangling with the effort.

He grunted something not understandable, as if he had tried to be kind and had met with a cold shoulder. Sometimes for two or three days after a drunk he would be soft and easy: but that only if you did not cross him.

"Supper ready?" he asked.

"No, it's not ready!" she answered with some bitterness.

"What in the hell is the matter with you?" he asked.

She was afraid of him. I had known that all my life. And I know now it was that fear which made her turn on me as I stood there poking my toes toward the feeble wave of heat.

"Mr. ten Hoor wanted you tonight," she said.

There was silence in the room, except for the popping of the fire, and that silence seemed to urge her on to something. "He promised to pay!"

"How much?" Papa said.

"Why, a quarter," she answered. "And it's not much work to it. Just be there. You can save enough for your foot. . . ."

"My foot can just stay crooked," I said. "I'm not going."

"Don't tell me what you'll do and won't do!" She nodded toward Papa. "I reckon you're gonna have to git aholt of him."

So he grabbed the bib of my overalls and led me, barefooted, into the yard where he found a stick, which seemed always handy for him; and he gave me a worse beating than usual, because I was determined not to cry even if he killed me. He must have sensed, finally, what I was up to, for he stopped abruptly and instead of going into the house he went off toward Mr. Acroft's barn.

I went into the house and carefully pushed the chair against the door behind me. My back felt as if it was plastered with a beehive, but I kept my face straight. Rudy was crying; huge tears, big as peas, rolled off his cheeks and splattered on the hearth. Mama sat with her shoulders drawn tight and her face buried in her hands. She spoke without lifting her face. "I know to my soul I have more trouble than any woman on earth. And you so stubborn you make him beat you like a mule."

"You told him to," I accused, "and you ought to know he didn't have any better sense than to do it. But you didn't care any more than he did."

For a minute there was silence. Then she said quietly, "Are you going?"

"Yes, and if it wasn't for Rudy I'd go and stay."

"Now, you let him hear you talking like that and he'll git aholt of you again."

"He's gone off somewhere," I said.

She asked if I wanted some clean clothes and I said yes. She brought clean underwear first and that set Rudy to laughing and crying at the same time, because he thought the whipping had caused me to ruin my clothes—which to him was both funny and sad. Finally, we were all laughing and I stripped off naked and let Rudy rub alcohol up and down my back. Within a few minutes I was on my way to The House.

Mr. ten Hoor was not surprised at my arrival. He was sitting in bed with a quilt over his feet and the old afghan about his shoulders. The light cast a grotesque shadow of him against the wall. Immediately he set about to explain my duties to me: fill the water pitcher, empty the basin, place a glass of water where he could reach it in the night, and so on. But the chief duty was something else and he explained it with some embarrassment: at exactly three-fifteen each morning his bowels moved; I was to arise immediately and carry his night chamber to the outhouse, some thirty yards below the building. For that I was to be paid a quarter.

So the days and the weeks passed and I began to like the new arrangement rather well. Somewhat to my surprise, Mr. ten Hoor was amazingly neat, agreeable though strict, and demanded nothing more than the fulfillment of my duties. I was never obliged to read longer than I chose, nor to talk if I wished to remain silent. In truth, he had an extraordinary ability to discern my feelings, and an extraordinary disposition in favoring them. I found many things inside the four walls of Mr. ten Hoor's world, and the first of them was a sense of order. "Tomorrow night," he would say, "we shall read 'The Lady or the Tiger.' You never read it, of course, well . . ." And "The Lady or the Tiger" hung on the curtain of tomorrow night like a bright star. I cannot say what he taught me: there were many things. One night he asked, "How are the rich treating you?"

"I don't know anybody that's rich," I answered.

"Let us say: the Acrofts."

"Oh, all right," I said. I had no intention of explaining the eruption between me and Vance. Furthermore, I had been exchanging, from time to time, pleasant conversations with Margo and Mrs. Acroft and Mr. Sid. Margo was unusually kind to me, which was not so much within itself, but was a great deal in view of other things.

"You are too young to understand," Mr. ten Hoor said, "but the rich devour the poor, and anything else that gets in their way. Remember that and it will save you a world of trouble."

Suddenly I said, "Was Vance mean—when you taught him?"

"Mean? No. He would be a Caesar or nothing. No, that's not the truth either. Only a part of it. When I first knew him he was an angel of the first order. Bright, certain, delicate. He was vain perhaps, but back of vanity is fire, and he had a fire burning in him which he didn't kindle himself. He was different. Apart. Above. It is sometimes a rich blessing to be one of the common herd. He was too bright, too certain. The others began to pick at him, accusing and teasing until at last he was labeled—I believe the appropriate word would be—a sissy. Great was the fall and great was the revolt. Or rather, the revolt came first. After that, he would be a Caesar. Only, well, he knew . . . he knew so well he was also a bit too delicate."

Mr. ten Hoor had turned pale; I felt he had said much more than he had intended.

"But why would he . . . ?"

"Why . . . why . . . why?" Mr. ten Hoor interrupted, and waved his hands as if to dismiss the matter forever.

Sometimes there would be mysterious sessions, strange conversations, during which Mr. ten Hoor would carry me into water well over my head. "Peace comes from within," he would say. "What rubbish, what artless reasoning. Comes from within! Sputum comes from within, and so does the human feces. Peace is a favorable converging of various lines of action and lines of thought. Why, I dare say it's more external than internal. Suppose this time tomorrow you failed to appear, and in your stead a message came saying you had been kicked in the head by Mr. Acroft's white stallion. Would I be at peace? No. Why? Because you had been kicked by a white stallion instead of a red one? No. Because you had been kicked instead of pawed? No. The answer: because it was *you* and not somebody whose name and face would be unfamiliar to me. Then a second message arrives, which informs me that you are safe and sound, save for a small scratch over the left ear. I am at peace again. Further, mind you. Suppose the second message does not reach me, I am not to be found, the lines cannot converge. Ah, *peace,* where are you?" And so on. I do not know whether his reasoning was clever; it was, nonetheless, food for me, whose diet had been a steady flow of grunts and nods and monosyllables, broken occasionally by a complete English sentence. So I feasted and was nourished, whether it was healthy or unhealthy.

Most mysterious things have a way of revealing their own mystery. Not Mr. ten Hoor. At the first sign of spring, he was exactly the same piece of obscure human machinery that he had been in the dead of winter.

Each Monday morning he paid me one dollar and seventy-five cents, and the business was transacted with considerable ceremony. He would take from his watch pocket a dollar bill, folded to the size of a postage stamp, and three quarters. He would seize my hand and shove these items into my palm, as if I had some notion of refusing his pay.

At home, we often talked about Mr. ten Hoor's money, suspecting he had thousands of dollars. It was strange to us that a man committed to the Poor Farm could hire and pay like a landlord. One explanation concerned a nephew or a niece in Oklahoma who liked Mr. ten Hoor and sent him ten dollars a month. Another report had it that he was well off and through some quirk of his nature preferred the Poor Farm for a home. Maybe both stories were true, or maybe both were false. Still, I got my dollar and seventy-five cents every Monday morning. I gave twenty-five cents to Rudy, twenty-five to Mama, and I kept twenty-five. The dollar I put each week in an old salmon can which fit very well against the wall, behind the meal and flour barrels. After the second week, I began to put my quarter in the can with the dollar, and Mama gave back her quarter. So the savings for the operation on my foot climbed at the rate of one fifty each week, and occasionally one seventy-five, for Rudy would sometimes give back his quarter, too.

For the rest of that winter and into the spring months of April and May, I had but one thought in mind: the day when I would have seventy-five dollars and could go to that doctor whom Aunt Pardy knew so much about and could demand a straight foot just as I might ask a shoe clerk for a particular type of shoe. Of course, even in my wildest notions, I did not suppose it was that simple. I understood there might be terrible pain and a long period of waiting for everything to be put right. But that was no matter. The important thing was the certainty that it could be done and would be done; and it would begin the day after my salmon can held seventy-five dollars. Such intense hope burned in me that I was a totally different person. There were times when I could not force a bite down my hungry throat, simply because I was transported by the thought of how things were going to be very soon. I would dream the clearest, most peaceful dreams showing this new vision of myself reconstructed in a perfect manner. When I would awake to reality I would always feel the keenest little arrows of disappointment. Quickly, however, the arrows would melt in the white flame of hope.

Hope is the strongest thing in this world, stronger than love. And in many respects it is the cruelest of the spiritual elements of this universe, a many-headed dragon whose heads multiply in defeat. For the very instant your soul's central wish lies dying in the ashes of ruin, that demon will raise his heads and tell you that tomorrow will be better. Tomorrow! Let tomorrow burn in the dragon's fiery flames; let him eat it and grow fat. I have no use for tomorrow, for there is no such thing: it is a cruel illusion which has bound a billion minds to eternal serfdom. Or a billion billion. What does it matter? It is past. I bought the universe with seventy-five dollars which I did not have but thought I was going to have.

As winter broke and spring came on I poked bill after bill and quarter after quarter into my salmon can, and waited. I passed my fifteenth birthday and for the first time in my life a birthday meant something to me. I was more alive than I had ever been. I was aware; I was thinking; I had faith. My eyes shone; even my hair brightened and my face became fuller and took on a healthier hue. Mr. ten Hoor noticed, and attributed all change to the mysterious work of the glands. One night, after reading, I stood before the wash-stand without a shirt and flexed my arms so that the muscles leaped rather convincingly. Mr. ten Hoor cried, "Splendid!" Which not only frightened me momentarily but brought Mrs. Clements to our door.

"Is anything wrong?" she asked.

"Wrong," Mr. ten Hoor said. "Look, madam, look! Have you ever seen a more splendid bust?"

Gazing at me and then at him, she said, "Why, Mr. ten Hoor, I do declare, if I didn't know you better I'd say you was being downright vulgar."

I was rather carried away by Mr. ten Hoor's observation, and I used it as fuel to feed the bright new light of hope burning in me. And the light in turn fed me. It shone through, like an early star, piercing the acres of darkness around my heart.

School was out and the crops were being planted. We worked from daylight until dusk, yet I did not mind. The day of salvation was not far away. It was just beyond the cotton crop. Last week the can held $17.25; next week: $19.00. And $75.00 was the price tag on the universe.

Summer wore on and we had a good crop under way. Actually, both the cotton and the corn looked better at that time of year than later on, when time came to gather. For the land we worked was tired and washed and unable to give forth very much. The rich land—the bottom sections—was reserved for Mr. Acroft and the tenants who had been with him ten or fifteen years. Papa plowed hard and he never got drunk more than three or four times that spring and summer, and each time they were short sprees, usually finished by late Sunday afternoon.

Mama and Rudy and I did all of our hoeing, and some of the hoeing for other tenants, who in turn plowed for us. On Sunday afternoons, Papa and the other tenants would some- times sit under the huge oak tree at the bridge below Mr.

Acroft's house, and Papa would brag about how clean his crops were and how much they would make. The other men would listen and nod and never dispute him, because they knew the land and knew it was not so and knew Papa would find out for himself soon enough. In June Papa said we would make twelve bales of cotton; in July he said ten; in August he said six; by September he quit saying, and we knew that one of his really big sprees was not far away.

I knew our crop would be slim, but I did not worry. My mind was filled with the Great Day ahead, and I had few, if any, misgivings. No, that is not exactly true. I did have one terrible week of fear, and that was caused by Vance too.

We had got along very well together that summer, chiefly because he was always on the verge of going somewhere and at such times he was agreeable and even friendly—you can get along with most anybody if he is getting ready to go somewhere. Two weeks he spent in Missouri visiting some of his mother's kin, and another week he went with Mr. Acroft to look at timber in Alabama and Georgia. Then there was a trip to a Y.M.C.A. camp and another trip to a Baptist camp in North Carolina. I don't remember any quarrels or unpleasantness to speak of, though that might be partially due to the hope which had brought me out of the shadows into the sunlight. But his trips were finally finished for the summer and the incident of the white stallion set us off again on the same old pattern.

I had understood from Margo and Vance and maybe half

a dozen others that the white stallion had once belonged to Vance. But when Vance had his trouble at school with Mr. ten Hoor, the stallion was taken away from him, and no one now was allowed to ride the stallion except Mr. Acroft. I suppose I was overly anxious to ride what was forbidden to Vance, and perhaps Mr. Acroft sensed my eagerness. One day in late August we were all in the fields trying to get the hay in the barn before the rain started when a clevis, or something, broke, and I was rushed to the store on the white stallion. Going, I was afraid and therefore careful; returning, I had lost my fears and so clung like a small brown lump above the fastest living thing I had ever seen in this world. That happened to be the day Vance returned from camp in North Carolina; and he happened to see me when the white mane was flying back in my face like a flag in a strong wind. Not that I cared. But I can understand how Vance felt when he saw me flying along on something which was once his own but was now forbidden to him, now that he was a fallen angel.

At the barn that night, after Mr. Acroft was gone, Vance asked me about the ride and asked how fast the stallion could run. He was so good natured about it, I said, "I made him fly. I really made him stretch out and fly."

"I reckon so," he said, "with that crooked foot jogging him in the side. That'd make a jenny run."

"It won't be crooked long," I protested. "I'm going to have it fixed. It don't cost but seventy-five dollars."

"Where would you get that much money?"

"That's all right. I've got nearly half of it now."

"You don't have to tell me where you got it. I'll find out."

"You might and you might not."

"If you're stealing it they'll catch you and put you in jail. How much did you say it cost?"

"Seventy-five dollars."

"Who said so?"

"That's all right who said so."

"They wouldn't cut your toenails off for seventy-five dollars."

"You don't know everything. You don't know about hospitals."

"I was born in one. Where were you born? In a barn? They wouldn't wash the rust off your ankles for seventy-five dollars."

"You're despise-able," I said.

"Despicable," he corrected. "But intelligent."

"If you was a bull in a concrete pasture, I'd . . ." There I hesitated, having forgotten, in my anger, the end of the statement.

"Why, you'd water and feed me. That's what you'd do." He threw back his head and laughed and said, "Moo!"

"I hate every gut in you," I said. "And someday I'll kill you as sure as God made little green apples, if you don't learn to leave me alone."

But the misery of that incident was not his laughing at me

nor his ugly joke. It was the thought that maybe he was right and seventy-five dollars would be a mere drop in the necessary pool. Every day I got out the money and poured it onto the table and counted it over and over again. It was just before cotton-picking time and Papa was at the house a lot, watching the crazy way I would count that money again and again. He was restless and nervous because there was no work going on, and every time I got out the money I would think: he is going to whip me if I do this again. I was afraid to ask Mama if the figure of seventy-five could be wrong, because she was so tired in those days she might have said Yes; and I was afraid to say anything to Papa, because he was so irritable and jumpy he would have, at best, put me to work at something. Rudy was the only one I could ask and he knew less than I. Of course, Mr. ten Hoor was a possibility, but I was beginning to be ashamed of having taken money from him and therefore shunned the matter in his presence.

I could hardly sleep, so anxious was I to refute the terrible doubt, malignantly increasing from day to day. But the middle of the week I made out a hospital bill of my own, which included bed, meals, ether, bandage, operation, medicine and nurses. I finally got everything itemized at a total cost of seventy-eight dollars, and as ether was the most mysterious of all the items I whacked it down three dollars and achieved the magic total of seventy-five. That satisfaction lasted until the tide of doubt could recede and flow back again, lashing with renewed energy. Then toward the end of the week, I hit on another idea. Suppose Vance was right. Suppose it would take ten times as much: seven hundred and fifty dollars instead of seventy-five. Well, I would spend ten years instead of one achieving my life's aim. After all, something so tremendous was not meant to be had in a few short months. How clever of me to work it all out by myself. I had the answer, final and irrevocable. I was at peace. I paid little attention to Papa, who came in that day with a handful of boll weevils crawling between his fingers and along his arm. He showed them to Mama and said, "They're ruining every boll."

She just looked at them and didn't say a word, as if that was what she had expected all along.

On Saturday Papa got drunk. He came home once with Mr. Emmett (they were friends again) and once he came home by himself, and each time he came by where I was chopping stove wood though he didn't say anything to me. Toward sundown he was still off somewhere so I quit chopping wood and went to the barn to feed. I had finished with everything but the hay when Vance came into the alley of the barn and called up to me, "I found out."

"What?"

"Where you got your money. You ought to be ashamed, taking money from a man in the Poor House, ready to fall in his grave. I'd be ashamed."

I didn't answer. I pulled the bale of hay closer to the edge of the loft.

"How much money you got?" he asked, and went on talking when he saw I was not going to answer. "You better pay me some mind. Your daddy's down at the bridge in a crap game with your money."

"You like to lie," I said.

He cried up at me, "Don't call me a liar, you grasshopping white trash. You're nothing but a tookel."

So I shoved that ninety-pound bale of hay over the edge of the loft and let it fall directly upon his head. It would have killed him, except it did not have far enough to fall. He lay in the powdery, clover-dust manure and the blood from his nose rushed down across the neat crease in the arm of his shirt. There were a few strange seconds of exultation when I thought he was dead. I do not remember climbing down. But I remember standing at the corner of the barn and watching him raise his shoulders a few inches and open his eyes. When he sat up, I walked off slowly toward our house.

I went through the kitchen door and before I had taken three steps I knew it was true. I rushed across the room and reached my hand desperately and wildly behind the meal and flour barrels. I backed away; I sat down, like something heavy falling in the middle of the floor. Rudy came and stood over me. "How come him to steal it?" he asked.

I made no attempt to answer. I just sat and shivered and looked at the August sun framed in the kitchen doorway.

Part Two

I

IT SEEMED to me that I had every reason to hate the Acrofts. They lived in a big white house whose front porch, in the summer, was almost covered with running roses. They had three fireplaces in the house and the greatest, warmest fires I have ever seen roared up those chimneys all winter long. They ate at a long table always loaded with food, and the Negro woman who moved quietly about handing dishes and filling glasses must have been the best cook in the world: for I remember nothing else like it.

I never ate at the Acroft table, but I know these things because I was sent there at all hours for one thing or another, usually for groceries. I would go into the kitchen and from the kitchen I could see the dining room. But sometimes I went through the front door and all the way back to the kitchen. I did this the first time in order to see what everything was like and maybe to get a glimpse of Vance's room. Afterward, I did it that way because I liked to walk through the house and smell it and look at the rich chairs and the pictures and the mirrors and the curtains trimmed in dark red and wade through the rugs.

I did go at all hours, but it seems to me they were always eating no matter what time I went there. And I could smell the coffee or the ham or the roast as far away as the lot gate. I am proud of one thing: I am proud I never sat down at their table. Sometimes I would go for something and when I started away, the Negro woman, named Pearl, would slip me a piece of steak or ham or fried chicken—never a word passed—and I would go off eating it. But I never sat down at their table. Yet, they always asked me to eat, and this is the way it was done:

I would stand in the kitchen, near the dining-room doorway, and tell Pearl I had come for coffee or lard or coal oil or whatever it was, and Vance would speak first: " 'Lo, Max."

I would answer and wonder if he was laying a trap for me, because he had actually got to be a little friendlier after I had pushed the bale of hay off on his head.

"Eat some supper," he would say.

I always answered him by shaking my head.

Then Mrs. Acroft would say, "Why, son, there's plenty."

And Margo never once said anything. She would simply look at me: that was all. I would stand there and wonder how much she knew. It seemed, of course, that she knew everything, how I had acted when Papa came home after he had got my money: I was still in the middle of the kitchen floor, as if struck with a malarial chill, when Papa came in, red at the throat, cursing Mr. Emmett and saying, "Where's my gun? I'll show that Blue-belly thief how to cheat me. . . ." A few seconds later he was gone and I got to my knees and began to pray; I prayed and prayed, mainly that he would get shot where his throat was reddest. "He won't git shot there," Rudy said calmly. "Well, anywhere," I said. "Oh, he won't git shot nowhere," Rudy said. And I quit praying.

Margo always sat at the table and looked as if she knew things like that. But then, a person who uses his eyes instead of his tongue always looks as if he knows a lot. And she never once asked me to eat.

But Mr. Acroft, or Mr. Sid—I called him Mr. Sid when I felt good toward him—would say nothing until the others had spoken and then he would break out with a good-natured scolding, because he evidently like to see anything eat heartily: "Come on, come on and eat. My god, boy, don't stand there with your stomach turning over and act bashful. If you act that-a-way you'll never get a wife. Grab you a chair and get busy. I know you're hungry."

I would think: Yessir, I am hungry and the water flows around my tongue and my stomach is talking, like a voice in a cave, but I will not eat at your table. Not one bite. Never. Because I hate you. Yet, I love you in a way too. Because you are able to take care of your own. They sit on either side of you and are not afraid. They know you will protect them against drouth and rain and cold weather and boll weevils and fate and the gods. You are strong and secure and you have big fires and plenty of food, but I am suddenly not hungry.

Now I must admit something which is the kind of thing that makes my face feel red in remembering, and it makes my scalp tingle unpleasantly; because at this distance I cannot say this was why or that was why. I am like a photographer who has to deliver a terribly unbecoming picture which happens to be a replica of the living model. And this thing had to do with the house of Acroft.

I had for some time quit going regularly to Mr. ten Hoor's. I would go when I felt like it and at other times I would do this mad thing which grew and grew on my brain. The Acroft house was splendid even in the daytime. First of all, it was huge and white. The windows were wide and tall, and from these at night there came such a dazzling abundance of light it seemed that a section of the Milky Way had been stored inside the house. That spectacle first burst on me one winter night when I hurried to the house to get corn meal for our supper.

As I was leaving I stood for a long time at the lot gate and stared at the brilliance and smelled the cured ham which Pearl was frying. I am sure I became drunk on the sight and smell, and that was what started me. Many nights when I was supposed to be in Mr. ten Hoor's room, I would be in the barn, lying on the hay, watching until the last Acroft light was extinguished. Then it would be too late to go home or to Mr. ten Hoor and so I would stay there all night, and I liked it. Sometimes in the early part of the night I would go stand in the shadows, between the fig trees and the smokehouse, and smell the odors from the kitchen. That went on for months, and it was the only thing I cared about. It kept something burning inside me just as the hope for a straightened foot had fired me on a year before. How many times I went I do not know. Two times, three times a week perhaps. And when I would miss a trip or two the following trip would seem all the more pleasant.

It was quiet in the barn, or rather, the noise of the mules and cows never disturbed me. I would lie there and consider the oddest subjects from the oddest angles imaginable. There I learned how to remake the world, and for all practicable purposes I owned the barn when the sun went down. I also lived years of my life ahead of time, with the advantage of reliving certain periods in which circumstances did not turn out just right. And finally, I learned to remember myself out of existence, which is perhaps the strangest of all feelings. For that, however, it was usually necessary to assume a fixed gaze upon a group of stars and drive the mind backward in time until the earliest remembered event existed on the other side of light, in darkness. Sometimes I could manage it by looking directly at the light flowing from the Acroft house, but it took longer that way, and it was easier to work with the stars. Two or three times Mr. Acroft came upon me at the barn at odd hours, but he never once asked what I wanted or why I was there. In his presence, I would think how strange it was that his barn showed more sense of order than our house.

It was during this mad period, on a dry September night, between my sixteenth and seventeenth year, that a second period, equally mad, commenced. I was supposed to be on my way to Mr. ten Hoor but instead I went to the barn and from there ventured as far as the smokehouse and stood in the shadows beside the fig trees. It was not a very dark night and I had a premonition that someone would see me. Supper must have been finished, for the noise came from the living room, but the smell of fried food was still on the air. It might have been that Pearl was cooking something for herself. I was standing still, listening to my own breathing, when I saw Margo come down the high back steps and go to the smokehouse. She had come to lock the house and that was all. Maybe she would never have seen me, for she had started back toward the steps and was not looking for anything. But I made some movement and spoke to her.

She was not startled, as almost any girl would have been. She was hardly surprised. She simply called my name and waited for whatever was to happen. When I made no further effort to move or to speak, she said, "What do you want?"

"Nothing," I said.

Then I stepped forward and caught her hand and held it in mine. Again she was not startled, and there was I am sure a faint response from her own fingers. It was madness that made me do such a thing, the same madness that put me beside the fig trees in the first place. But it was done; the wheel was spinning; and so I said, "I like you. You're not like the others."

She answered nothing. On her face was the same puzzled, quiet expression as when the others would ask me to sit down at their table and eat. For a few seconds our fingers remained locked together. Then she slipped her hand away and ran up the steps into the house. At the kitchen door she made the briefest pause and looked back before entering.

For a minute or two I waited around in utter confusion. I even entertained some notion that Mr. Acroft might come out with his rifle and I would have nothing to protect me but the bare branches of the fig trees. I started for the barn, and then for home, and finally I decided to go to Mr. ten Hoor's.

I had not been to his room for a week, and when I entered the details of the room seemed only vaguely familiar: like the fleeting, insecure feeling of this-has-happened-to-me-before, in another lifetime. Before I knew what was happening, Mr. ten Hoor was laughing at me, while I gripped the brass footrail and stared at him. There was hurt in his eyes and suddenly I understood something which made me cold and warm in the same breath: I was the only one in the world who could make Mr. ten Hoor happy or unhappy. All other things were past; all other times and memories were forgotten or filed away. He was in my hands and he would be there until the earth gave way beneath him. Then the laugh, which was also both cold and warm, ended and he looked at me sternly.

"Where have you been?"

"Lots of places."

"Lots of places! What an answer! Totally unpoetic, devoid of beauty, and I've spent months teaching you the basic concepts of poetry and beauty. Where have you been? I've been in the hill and dale. I've been to Hillandale. Couldn't you think of that? Or has the cat got your mind? You run off to heavens knows where and leave me to roost in the stink of my own excrement. Don't you know you've spoiled me? Two days: all right. Three days: all right. Four days: maybe. But a week. Why did you have to be gone a week? What engrossing business, huh? What . . . ? I'll unravel this mystery. . . ." I could see he was talking himself into a good humor. The lines around his eyes had fallen a bit, and I could see a teasing expression creep over his face.

"The prodigal has returned," I said, remembering the time we had discussed the parable with great care. "Where is the fatted calf?"

"Prodigal! Fatted calf! Ah, yes. The work of a stupid, indulgent father. I am neither stupid nor indulgent. If I were the pontiff I would have you crawl unclothed through a blackberry thicket until your flesh was a living, bleeding example to those who would ignore schedule and duty. And if you whined, if you so much as uttered one whimper, I would excommunicate you." Then he drew himself together again, like a serpent preparing to strike, and demanded, "Where in heaven's name *have* you been?"

"Places."

"Far places, I gather. Too far away to send any word or message."

"If you wanted to know bad, why didn't you ask Mama?"

"You listen to me. Yesterday evening, at or about six thirty-four of the clock, I inquired of your whereabouts from your mother. I understood you had been here every night this week. Here! On duty! Would you be kind enough to exorcise this ghost, or must I do it?"

"I don't believe in ghosts," I said.

"But I do. I shall thrust my invisible dagger into the invisible flesh. *En garde!* All right. Here it comes: *Cherchez la femme!*" A great peal of laughter escaped his lips; a ringing, resounding explosion, which I thought was the healthiest sound I had heard in that house.

"You're crazy," I said.

"*Cherchez la femme!*" he cried, and the laughter came out again, exactly the same way but with less volume.

Then Mrs. Clements opened the door, without knocking, and said: "Do tell, Mr. ten Hoor, but you must be having a party in here."

"*Cherchez la femme!*" Mr. ten Hoor cried.

"What *are* you two boys up to?" Mrs. Clements said, and she tried to repeat the words, *Cherchez la femme.* "Why, Mr. ten Hoor, you sound for all the world like a turkey gobbler."

"We're looking for the woman," Mr. ten Hoor said.

"What woman?"

"The woman in this mystery. The French are wise people. They always say: *Cherchez la femme:* Look for the woman."

"Is this woman you're looking fer French?"

"Hardly, Mrs. Clements."

"Well, how'd the French git mixed up in it? And what is it anyway, a riddle?"

"No, madam. A mystery."

"Oh, you!" she cried, aggravated and hurt. She went back to her room.

Mr. ten Hoor waited for me to say something, and finally I said, "You're strange."

"Perhaps," he answered. "The mentality of a genius and the desires of a child. But you're not side-tracking me. Who is she? This creature you've been chasing and apparently caught? Margo?"

"Yes."

"An Acroft!" he said. "Unfortunate. Stare at me then. You're a clever lad. You think misfortune always comes in an ugly bundle. You're mistaken. Sometimes it comes wrapped like a Christmas package. Don't ask me how I know these things. It was a long way from the snip of the umbilical cord to the click of that doorbolt when I first entered this room—a long way in miles and years and faces. From a vast patchwork of experience I warn you to leave them alone."

"The Acrofts?"

"The Acrofts."

"Margo's not like the others."

"Phewt! An Acroft is an Acroft! You hear me, don't you?" It was then I first saw Mr. ten Hoor lose control of himself. He was speechless for a few seconds and his face turned red, like a high-school senior in panic over a forgotten vale-dictory. "It's a solemn warning. You leave them alone."

"I'm not going to bother them."

"Don't pretend to misunderstand me," he said.

But at that moment I was not ready to turn my back on the Acrofts; I was not prepared for the warning; I was not prepared for anything, because at that moment I was throw-ing the dark past away like so much dishwater thrown from the kitchen door into the back yard. "Mr. Sid is good to me," I said, and my mind began to count off the things he had done and the times he had been very friendly with me.

Mr. ten Hoor clouded his face and said, "Oh, Jerusalem, Jerusalem, how oft would I have gathered you under my wing, but you would not. . . ."

I merely stared at him.

He said, "The Acrofts will devour you."

"Let them," I answered.

"They will pick you like a headless chicken and singe you and laugh at the smell of scorched flesh. With exceptional pleasure too, because you are exceptional."

"You just don't like them."

"Like them! I hate the rich. Detest them. They hold on

and hold on and hold on, because they're afraid. And in the end somebody gets stifled, choked blue. Somebody else, of course. Somebody about like you."

I didn't stay with Mr. ten Hoor that night. I went home. But on the way I stopped by the Acroft house and waited and waited until every light was out. I knew then I was getting deeper and deeper into something I had better stay out of, but I cannot honestly say now whether I was afraid.

2

I WAS seventeen that winter and my foot was still crooked and our house was still cold and Mama still coughed hard and cooked long hours and Papa still went to the saw-mill and got drunk when he got ready and Rudy still missed days of school because of his legs. Counted up, we had been on the Acroft place two years and two months. The world had not changed, but I thought it had.

I was in high school, for even the poorest, the lowest, the stupidest of all our horde who move from farm to farm like grasshoppers can go to school free or nearly so. From grammar school to high school was a big thing for me, but that was not why I thought the world had changed.

I know from being in the war that unbelievable things can happen right before your eyes. You may search the skies for the enemy and at the very moment of intense concentration, in the very direction you are looking, a plane may loom out of nowhere and strafe you and be gone before you can open your mouth. Recounting the incident, you may think you saw it when it was no larger than a mosquito on the horizon, when the truth is it was past you and gone before you got a good look.

There is a moment of not seeing and a moment of seeing, a moment of not knowing and a moment of knowing, but who can point his finger and say here it is, anchored in time between eight-thirty-one and eight-thirty-three, on this day or that day? At least, you can not do such a thing in the matter of love. I was seventeen and I loved someone and the world was different.

Yes, I should have hated the Acrofts. That was one side of it. They had thick rugs and soft chairs and bright lights and good clothes and lots of food and big roaring fires. They walked across the earth in a different way, because they owned it—part of it—while not a handful belonged to me. And the other side: they still asked me to sit at their table; they furnished us month after month, though we owed five hundred and forty-four dollars two years from the day we moved there; they let me use Mr. Sid's typewriter one day; and most of all nobody said a word when I began to pay special attention to Margo, and maybe nobody even noticed.

In those days I would get mad at myself. I would say: *why do you have to be such a fool?* It is nothing and it will come to nothing, and the least you can do is not let them make a fool out of you. Tonight I will stay here in the house and will not budge one inch toward the Acrofts; I will forget them. I will forget the lights and the smell of good food. I will forget she ever touched my hand, ever looked at me, ever spoke a word in my presence. So it was settled. Yes.

For a fraction of one minute.

I could pretend we were out of coal oil. That would get me in the house and maybe into her presence. And—shivering heart—she might be the one who would go with me from the house across fifty steps of darkness to the coal-oil tank locked in the smokehouse shed. Shivering heart! It was silly.

Yes. And pure madness.

But real as the smell of coal oil.

I would invent excuses to go there and when there were no excuses to be invented, I would go anyway and stand near the smokehouse and think how near I was to something rooted in my heart. I began to like the house and the rugs and the people in that house, even Vance. I took what he said and let it slide off me like so much hail rolling down a tin roof. I would take anything that winter, if I had a chance to stand before one of Mr. Sid's roaring fires and have a few words with Margo. What words? Any words. And that's a thing nobody understands, and a thing that hurts too and tears you to pieces. I would lie in bed long after Rudy was asleep and wonder: what excuse will I have to go there tomorrow night? What will they think? And even if I find a reason for tomorrow, what about the day after?

But that was not all of it, not even the worst part. I had daily—or hourly for that matter—to consider what was in her mind. Maybe she liked me, maybe she didn't. When I was lowest and knew that it was a joke even to hope for what I hoped for, then I would remember things like the time about the paper. I said to her, standing there before their hearth, with the room warm and the fire roaring, "I want to borrow some paper."

She handed me a package, forty or fifty sheets, and I said, "I'll take five sheets if you don't care."

"I wouldn't care if you took it all," she said. What that meant to me! I guess Mr. ten Hoor would have said, "Crumbs. They are feeding you crumbs. What's more, she's not too pretty." Maybe she was pretty and maybe she wasn't. I don't care. To me she was beautiful and good and perfect as a star. Sometimes I would absolutely want to die.

Say one thing for me. Say I went as clean as a lightning rod and washed my own clothes every night and ironed them myself if Mama didn't have the time or was too tired; and stood in the washtub every night of the world in water freezing cold by the time I got it as high as my armpits and scrubbed my skin until it looked as if I had been stung all over.

Say that Mama noticed, and Rudy too.

Finally there was Vance, right in the Acroft living room,

and I was caught and he knew it. Of course, he knew it to begin with.

"Margo's not here," he said.

"Well," I answered, trying to suggest it could not possibly matter to me where she was.

"Mother and Papa took her to town to get her some new clothes. They're going to send her to Aunt Edna's—in Missouri."

"What for?"

"To get her away from you. Stupid!"

A coal of fire might as well have popped onto my tongue and slid down my throat; and in so doing seared all my vocal cords.

"Look at you! Look at you!" he cried, and then he literally lay down on the floor and rolled in his own laughter. When he quieted himself he lay on his back and looked up at me. "I can tell you something'll be good for your body and soul."

"What?"

"Some advice."

"I'm listening."

"It won't do you any good, the way you take on over Margo."

"They're not sending her anywhere," I said, finally catching on after his joke had seared me.

"They won't have to. Papa will tend to you."

"Yeah? I reckon he'll chop my arms off just below the elbow."

"Not that. But he'll tend to you well enough."

"I reckon he'll eat me, because he's rich and the rich *devour* sharecroppers like us. We can't talk and can't figure and don't eat good and don't wear much, but we like what we like and we hate what we hate. And I hate every cell in you!"

"And Margo . . ." He was laughing at me. "What do you say about her? Has she tried to devour you?"

"You think you're higher than the North Pole, but somebody will saw you down!"

"And Margo?" He let out again with his ridiculous laughing and I thought of taking a chair and whacking him square across the head, but my knees had got weak for some reason and I could hardly stand. Suddenly he got up and straightened his face and assumed his familiar air of being old and wise. "I've warned you but personally I don't care."

"Don't care for what?"

"I don't care if you marry her and raise a whole litter of little Harpers."

He was way ahead of me, and the word *marry* hit me like a solid object and made me realize how absurd were some of the things I had done. First in my mind was the wish to love and right behind that was the wish to be loved, and I never got any further than that, until Vance came probing along. The thing he did was to open the floodgates for another tidal wave of hope, and I began again (as when I thought my foot would be put straight) the long, cruel climb up the stairway, at the top of which one expects to have the world under command.

If the hope of having a healthy, normal foot was one drop, then this new thing (which Vance had implanted) was an ocean of joy or sorrow, depending on whether I was up or down. Sometimes I was so full of faith in the future (What if it was two years or ten years?) that I could not put my mind on any problem for more than one minute. $A^2 - B^2 = (A - B) (A +$ yesterday she said: I'll be glad when March is over. I hate the wind.)

The first warm breath of spring came and my heart had not yet torn its way through my ribs. A miracle, I thought, being in the mood to believe in the miraculous. Great rivers of sunlight poured over the hills and life leaped and I was unseasonably happy. We started a new crop, which alone gives rise to too much hope. And there was wood smoke— flocks of birds returning and buttercups in every yard. The inside ankle of my right foot was raw where my left shoe toe had scraped again and again, but I hardly noticed, and kept on with the plowing as if the harvest would be mine. When it was warmer I pulled off my shoes.

Then one day when the sun was bright and the water cool we stood alone in the shallow creek: I have never known another moment like it. I was there first. I left my hat and shirt on the plow handles, gave my pants' legs two or three rolls, scooted down the bank and stood in six or eight inches of water and looked up and saw her when I thought nobody was closer than a mile. I was sorry I did not have on my shirt and then I was not sorry and before a minute passed I didn't know what I thought; but I felt a tremendous wave of good fortune because my left foot was buried in the water. It was like being asked a difficult and obscure question, which by chance you can answer. Only a thousand times more important. I said nothing and she said nothing, but she pulled off her sandals and gave out a childish cry when the water rushed across her bare feet.

There I stood whole—with my foot buried—and her eyes were on me, like the sun, and I wished to be carried up, like smoke, until I was nothing in the universe. It was almost more than I could stand: that is, I was afraid my mind might come apart like willow fuzz and I would start talking or acting in sheer madness.

The sand was dry to the very edge of the water and I sat down, keeping my foot buried and keeping my eyes not on her face but on her bright print dress which seemed as near as my own breath and far away as a rainbow.

Nobody asked her. Nobody said a word. She came and sat down beside me and we buried our hands in the sand. I remember the feel of our fingers, hidden, locked together. I remember our faces close together. I will remember until I am nothing: the sunlight, the water, the smell of her hair, the sound of her whispering, "Something caught our pigeons in the barn." Such things are never finished; they go away and they come back, like the stars.

That night I sood before the mirror of our old dresser and asked: Why did she do that? There was no water to hide my foot and no sunlight and no universe of blue sky to make me feel big and secure. But I had faith: a little in myself and a lot in her. I pulled off my shirt and dropped it around my left foot, which was almost the same as standing in water. I looked at myself closely and I tell you it was not too bad at all. I was surprised. I was really more than surprised. My body had filled out miraculously and the sun had added a healthy touch of color. My face was serious—old, I thought—and determined and rather well shaped. Once my chin had been too sharp and my nose too long, but now those flaws had disappeared. My eyes were bright, bluer than ever before in my life; my teeth were clean and shining and straighter than ever before. I was looking at my hair, wondering if it was brighter, when Rudy caught me. Or rather, that was when I saw him. How long he had been watching me, I don't know. I felt very foolish and waited for him to say something which would make me feel worse.

"Buddy?"

"What?" I said rather sharply.

"If you was to have your foot fixed, you'd be good-looking as nearly anybody."

"Pshaw!" I said.

"You're stouter than Vance. You're big. I mean, like here." He squeezed the muscle of his arm.

"Pshaw!" I said, and flexed my right arm the best I could.

"Make a frog."

I showed off. I made a frog on my muscle and Rudy was delighted. I mention such a slight incident because it is important to me: it was one of the last things I ever did for him.

I went to Mr. ten Hoor's and spent the night and he gave me the usual quarter, with which I meant to buy something for Rudy because he had said those things. But I never got to buy anything. The last kind act I would ever do for Rudy on this earth was finished. Wherever he is I wonder if he knows the quarter in my pocket that morning was to be spent for him. I wonder if he knows he held a place in my heart that not even Margo could touch; and I wonder if he heard when I used to pray that he would never throughout eternity remember a single unkind thing I had done or said to him. Sweet, innocent brother, I wish it had been me that morning instead of you.

3

I HAVE often wished I might have spent that last night with Rudy. He could wake up happier than anybody I have ever seen, and he could do it with rain beating on the roof and icy slivers of the wind pressing through the cracks. He would stand almost naked; not a shiver would move him;

and the next second he would be in his overalls, looking so warm that I would get up enough courage to push back the quilts and jump out beside him. I wish I had been there that last morning, so I might have seen for myself and judged whether some premonition warned him he was in the last hours of his life. Maybe it is the old, old feeling: if I had been there things might have been different.

Mama said he acted strange that morning. But what else was there for her to say? And after it was over, what else was there for her to see in remembering? They had got up at three-thirty, according to Mama. A few minutes later, Rudy came into the kitchen and stood by the table until breakfast was ready. He said nothing until he asked for a sugared biscuit. Now, sugared biscuits are what I like. Rudy never liked them. But there he was asking for a sugared biscuit and Mama fixed it, and then he asked for another. He stood while he ate, and Mama said he was far away all the time. Then he went silently out into the bright, life-swollen morning to die.

I remember the day above all the days of my life: like some omnipotent hammer coming down on a gigantic nail and burying it with one merciless stroke. And whatever I say about Mr. Acroft, whether I hate him or love him, I remember him that day as I would remember a chimney where a house has burned.

I had got up at four o'clock. I cleaned Mr. ten Hoor's room in a very few minutes, and while it was not like him to be talkative in the mornings, I do remember we had an unusually long conversation. "I like this time of morning," he said, "and this time of year, because sometimes I am able to imagine I'm a new baby just coming into the world."

"Would you like to be my age?" I asked.

"My dear little brutal lad! Would I like to be your age? I want to *be*, whether it's your age or Methuselah's. And while you're being so cruel, remember you're only a step behind me. As the years go by that step will get shorter and shorter."

"I didn't mean it that way," I said.

"You're too young to know what you meant. Seventeen! It sounds like *Christmas* sounded when I was four. Plenty of time ago. But you . . . youth doesn't believe in time, or that green apples will give you the bellyache, or that this whole miserable and pitiful horde of us from the whitest to the blackest, from the richest to the poorest will be dust and ashes a little more than one hundred years from this very morning. You can't conceive of a hundred years, can you? No. But I can. If you've eaten three quarters of an apple you ought to know what the rest would taste like. I am speaking about life. Do you know what life is like to me?"

"No."

"It's like a horn, tiny at one end and infinite at the other. A great deal depends on which end of the horn you enter. Not so much what's in the horn. Rich man, poor man, beggarman, thief; doctor, lawyer, merchant, chief: each must drink so much sorrow, one from a gourd, another from a china teacup."

"A gourd holds more. Do you mean . . . ?"

"Don't interrupt me!"

"I've got to go," I said.

"No, you don't have to go. I'm going to read you a poem."

"Before breakfast?"

"Great poetry will stand a reading at noon, midnight, *or* dawn, and don't you be one to doubt its efficacy. Now you lend me your ears:

> Peppermint sticks
> And coal oil wicks,
> And Santa down the chimney;
> He walks so light,
> In the middle of the night:
> Up and see what he gimme.
>
> The scaly bark tree
> And hickory tea,
> And I'm too old for Christmas;
> When I get grown
> I'll take what I own
> And travel to the Isthmus
> Of Anywhere,
> Or Nowhere,
> Or maybe far
> As Kra.
>
> Twickenham place
> And Western Thrace,
> The rock of great Gibraltar,

> The Mount of Zeus,
> And Syracuse,
> Kankakee and Kalmar.
>
> Afghanistan
> And Akkerman:
> If not today, tomorrow:
> You'll meet her there
> Or meet her here,
> A lady known as sorrow.
> Oh, Anywhere,
> Or Nowhere,
> Or maybe far
> As Kra.

Only after he had finished did I notice he was reading from a paper and not from memory. Where the paper came from I do not know. Maybe he kept it under his pillow or in the pocket of his night shirt. I paid no attention at the time, but for politeness I asked, "What do you call it?"

"I call it, 'Lines Composed Too Many Years Below the Bridge of Accountability.' "

He gave me the sheet of paper, the lines set down in his own small handwriting, and I kept it for years. I had it that morning as I hurried toward the barn, without breakfast, because I was late and I knew Papa would be mad. I trotted along, hungry, willing to trade all the verse in my head for something to fill my stomach.

Nevertheless, I was not feeling low. I planned to show Margo Mr. ten Hoor's verse, which would provide common ground between us for a few minutes; and any plan of that sort always lifted my spirits considerably. When you are in love, every action around you bears directly toward the beloved: I must tell her this, I must show her that, I must ask her of such and such, I must give her Mr. ten Hoor's poem. Oh, I have come to understand such things, and my heart leaps less quickly, less surely. I have seen strange things happen and have failed to wonder more than momentarily. But why, of all the mornings of my life, why did Mr. ten Hoor choose that morning to give me some lines which said:

> If not today, tomorrow:
> You'll meet her there
> Or meet her here,
> A lady known as sorrow.

And he had never before given me any kind of lines.

So the world spins on. We made our crop, and I have long since forgotten how many bales it was or how many bushels of corn, or how much we owed Mr. Acroft at the end of the year. But I can see Rudy walking down the long alley of that barn with a bridle in his hand.

When I got to the barn the sun was just breaking the rim of the horizon. Everywhere there was birdsong and the smell of fresh earth and wood smoke and mules. From the pond, I saw Vance standing by the gear shed and when I got closer I heard Mr. Sid tell him to harness a new mule named Yancey, which Mr. Sid had bought from a man named Go Jones. Vance said something which I did not hear. I simply know he answered something and remained exactly where he was. I thought he said, "I'm afraid of that mule." But he later denied saying anything.

Just as I reached the gear shed, I heard Papa say to Rudy, "Don't stand there! You can harness that mule!" It was a harsh, stubborn voice, full of resentment and bitterness and meanness. It was the same voice I had been hearing for years, the same cold cruel barking that made us run when we could have walked, that woke us up when we might as well have slept. Because we were sharecroppers, hungry and ignorant, grasshopping from farm to farm, there was still no reason one of us had to harness a mule for Vance Acroft, heir apparent to the throne. But Papa was that way about things. He licked their boots and then he was hateful to us because he had a sorry taste in his mouth. And this is the thing that hurts my heart: one man had sense and consideration and kindness enough to protect his son; the other man did not. Oh, he was little and mean and ignorant; and when it was done he quickly washed his hands of the whole affair: it was in no part his fault. Nothing preyed on his mind; he lost no sleep, after the first night; he didn't even get drunk. When Mr. Acroft said, "You shouldn't have sent the kid in there," he answered cool as a judge, "Well, that couldn't be helped." I suppose it couldn't. I suppose nothing can be helped, and for that reason I cannot help hating sometimes.

I saw it all. I saw Rudy unhook the chain, open the stable door, step across the sill. I saw the mule whirl, quicker than a heartbeat; it was deadly as lightning. The print of one mule shoe was on his forehead and he was stretched out in the alley as still as hay, his hand clutching the bridle, his last link between here and eternity.

The birdsong stopped, the wood smoke settled, the skies darkened. I knelt in the dry manure and held on to a handful and waited for the world to end. There was no world without him. I put my hand in my pocket and gripped the quarter tighter and tighter, until at last my voice came to me and I uttered a horrible cry. All that was done, and still I was the first to him. But he never knew, and so it does not matter who was first.

How quickly men can gather! It seems to me I had no sooner touched the hand that held the bridle than a dozen men were about us—and some had come a mile, or two miles. I had not looked up but I knew they were there; I saw their shoes and knew. And I heard one of them say with a trace of disappointment, "I thought hit was the one with the crippled foot."

People whom I had never seen before, or did not remember seeing, flocked to our house, and almost all of them brought food, most of it sweet stuffs. Among the pies and the cakes and the brownies, there were nine egg custards, which happened to be what Rudy liked best. I could not touch a bite of it. But there were people who did eat heartily, people who were not used to pies and cakes; and I was glad they could eat. Late in the afternoon I was alone with Mama in my and Rudy's room—it must have been the only time in that whole twenty-four hours that I was alone with her—and she said, "Did you see the custards? And he liked them so much."

"I remember."

"If he could be brought back . . . to enjoy just one . . . I'd be satisfied."

"I wouldn't be satisfied."

"I didn't mean that. I wanted all my children to outlive me. I wanted . . ." Then a woman came in to stop our talk. It was Mrs. Jones, the wife of the man who had owned the mule a short week ago. She sat on the bed and cried and told how she had warned Go, her husband, but she had no idea he would trade the mule to a neighbor, and a close neighbor at that.

"It might as well be my child as anybody's," Mama said.

The woman got up and left.

So many people had arrived I thought the house would fall through. I guess it was not a lot of people, but it seemed like a lot to me then. Children cried to see Rudy, and once every hour or two, mothers had to take them in and hold them up. That went on all day and all night.

Margo came at dark. She nodded to me and that was all that passed between us. She sat by her father, who had been there all day attending to everything. For a long time I sat where I could watch her. But sometime in the night she left, and I never knew when.

The people stayed on and on. They talked low or whispered and sometimes there would be a stir of quiet laughter. If any good came out of the whole matter it was that people seemed a little kinder to each other. Which was a great price for Rudy to pay, alone.

4

Within three or four days we were going on with the plowing and planting almost as if nothing had happened. I do not mean I had forgotten—I will never forget—but almost within a matter of hours I had accepted the everlasting element which had crossed our paths. And everlastingness is the hardest thing for me to understand, no matter in what form it appears. I had looked down the endless corridor of eternity and when I turned my eyes away I felt wiser and stronger and older. Also, I no longer hoped for so much: I supposed I would live my days out with my left foot twisted and eternally scraping against my right ankle. So in this life it seems that when you get set for one thing another happens.

About a week after the funeral, a man named Luke Shakelford came to our house one night. He came at night, he said, because he didn't want to stir up trouble. I was already in bed, and although I got up and came to the door to listen I didn't hear everything. But I must have heard the theme of Mr. Shakelford's talk four or five times: "Now, if you want to sue Acroft he won't have a leg to stand on."

I'll have to hand it to Papa that he kept saying, "I don't know about that, Mister." And when Mr. Shakelford left, he said, "I just want you to get it straight I'm not here to egg on a thing. I make a pretty decent living practicing law, without chasing after ambulances. If you want to bring suit, it won't cost you a penny if we lose. In any case, I wish you wouldn't say anything about my coming out here. It's your decision. When you decide what you want to do, just let me know."

When the lawyer was gone, we all gathered on the hearth as if it was freezing weather, and looked at each other and wondered about this new turn in our lives. It was enough to make us wonder, for the man had once or twice mentioned twenty thousand dollars.

"It won't do," Mama said. "I won't take money over my boy's grave like that."

"You can't tell," Papa said. "It might work."

I was startled. I had never heard of a sharecropper suing anything but a railroad. We pulled up chairs and sat around the hearth for a while, all silent. Then we went to bed, and the suit was not mentioned again for a few days. The next I heard of it was from Vance. We happened to be at the barn together after the others were gone, and he said, "I hear your old man's going to sue us."

I was surprised, of course, and all I could answer was, "I wouldn't know about that."

"It's about like a Shardy," he said, Shardy being his peculiar name for a sharecropper. "We feed you and clothe you and take care of you, and then when something happens you want to sue us."

"You're a coward!" I cried out. "If you wasn't such a miserable coward you woulda gone in the stable and got your brains kicked out instead of Rudy's. I despise you!"

"There's no love lost."

We crept toward each other like animals. I could feel my heart beating fast because I knew I would have my hands full, maybe too full. Vance read his books and quoted Shakespeare better than Mr. ten Hoor and banged out tunes on the piano, but he was no weakling. I didn't go into him with the idea of victory at the first blow; I was fighting him chiefly because I thought he had let Rudy pay a price for him, and he was not too much concerned with the sacrifice. We were Shardies, in his eyes, and it was our business to pay and sacrifice. So I would make it my business to jar some sense into his head.

I do not remember the fight so much as what happened when it was over. Still, the fight itself was long and bitter and bloody and I matched him, for a while anyway, blow for blow, maybe because I was full of hate and he was not. I was the first to score a knockdown, with my right hand strangely enough—I am left-handed. He came up furiously and knocked me down twice before I could recover my sense of direction and again knock him down with some wild swinging of my right fist. By then we were ready to go at it a little less savagely, and three or four minutes went by with no more than three or four blows landing. We were stalling, giving ourselves a chance to talk.

"Son, you'll have to eat some more cornbread and molasses before you can handle me," Vance said.

"I'll be there when you are."

"No, Max, you'll never get there. You're a Shardy and you'll be late all your life. Here. Eat some of this." He flung a small handful of manure into my face.

"I'll kill you," I said, evenly and calmly.

"When? Now?"

We were at each other again, and though there were no knockdowns I believe the second round was more ferocious than the first. Finally, we found ourselves separated by a few yards, and each waited for the other to move in for the final victory. Both were exhausted, both bled like butchered hogs. It had passed the stage of playground fighting and had become mortal enemy against mortal enemy. Therefore, we proceeded more cautiously. The end came rather quickly. He hit me somewhere on the chin, not a very hard blow, and I crumpled back against a stable door. I knew what was going on but my legs were too weak to move me. I started to get up when I saw Mr. Acroft come out of nowhere and seize Vance by the shoulder. It seemed to me his powerful hand actually lifted Vance off his feet and turned him half around. "What in God's name are you two doing?"

I saw with some pleasure that blood was running from the corner of Vance's mouth, his chin was cut, his left eye almost closed. Mr. Acroft shook Vance, as if his answer had not come quick enough.

"I reckon we were fighting."

"What about?" Mr. Acroft asked.

"About me being me and him being him. I reckon that's the main reason."

"Both of you ought to be ashamed of yourselves. We've had enough happen in this barn already."

"I'm ashamed that it took me so long to whip him," Vance said.

Mr. Acroft grabbed his shoulder again and I could see Vance flinch. "You're talking to me now, boy. Do you understand that? See if you can find your way to the house."

Mr. Acroft waited a few seconds, as if he had something to say to me. But he just looked, not with harshness nor kindness, and turned and followed Vance, who turned (the moment Mr. Acroft passed him) and thumbed his ears at me, which was another way of calling me a Shardy.

I was so angry the tears rolled down my cheeks. I sat not three yards from where Rudy had fallen, and before I knew it I was talking quietly: "Rudy, you listen to me. I will kill him. I will kill him because he killed you. He was a coward and you were brave. He's not even sorry for it. He thinks he owns everything in sight, but he'll see. Rudy, I will. One day I will. Mr. Sid is different—I can tell. But Vance is not even sorry about you, and I'm going to kill him. . . ."

When I finally got up and started for home, I saw Margo in their garden. I stopped and watched her, bareheaded, bare-armed, gathering an apronful of something: lettuce? carrots? onions? radishes? How much I wanted to know! A moment ago I had thought all feeling in me was gone, and now the springs had refilled to overflowing. How could *he* be your brother? I thought. It was almost dark. I called hello to her. She straightened and said, "Hello, Max," and I thought the sound of her voice carried on and on around the world.

I started on home. Everything was so tangled up I could not see the end of anything. There were Margo and Vance and my vow and my foot and Mama's spells of coughing and Papa's talk about a trial; so what would become of us? When I got to the creek I buried my foot in the water and looked back at the Acroft house, which had been lighted by them. I was thinking: she is in this place or that place, she is doing this or that, she is saying such and such. All at once I looked down at the water that covered my foot and I whispered, "Rudy, listen . . . I wish it had been me. . . ."

5

ONE SATURDAY night Papa came in drunk and said he was going to sue the Acrofts for a million dollars. When he got sober he changed it to twenty thousand and we knew he meant it. Mama was down and out about the matter, and she argued how it wasn't right and no good could come of it. "I never had no money," she said, "and never expect to have none, and plain don't want none coming over my boy's grave like that."

Papa would sit before the hearth, like it was cold and there was a fire, and he would stretch out his legs and spend the money. "Now here's what I'd do with it. I'd buy me a sawmill and a tract of timber and maybe you think I wouldn't be setting on top of the world. I figure . . ."

"You ain't got it yet," Mama would say.

"Now you hush! I figure . . ."

"And you ain't gonna git it. . . ."

"Will you hush?"

"Because the Lord never meant folks to take money over a body's grave. My own boy . . . I'd starve and go ragged."

The red would be oozing down Papa's face. He couldn't stand the contradictions any longer. He would get up and pace around nervously. "You ain't fer from ragged now, sister."

"And not fer from starving," she would add, and he would see she had beat him to something.

"You're never with me," he would say. "Just looks like it's in you to go east if I go west. Well, sister, I may take my hat and head out west fer good someday."

"Well, brother, you know where it's hanging."

Sometimes he would curse a while and ask Mama what had got into her and if she thought more of Sid Acroft than she thought of him. Mama said once, "Why, I reckon Sid Acroft is a good man."

"I didn't ask you if he was a good man. I said do you think more of him?"

"I don't think none too serious about nobody, cause you never can tell what a body will come to."

"Me! Me!" Papa almost screamed, and the red was oozing again. "I'm asking about me!"

"Why, everybody knows they ain't much to you, Ludie."

I thought he might throw a chair, or get the gun, but he didn't do a thing except sit down and seal his lips and stare into the empty fireplace. That was all for that night, but in a day or two he was spending the money again.

He spent the money all summer long: for a sawmill, for a farm, for a filling station, for whatever came to his mind. And in spite of those arguments he was pleasanter than he ever was before. Sometimes we would go two or three days

without his fussing at me, and sometimes we would stop in
the shade to rest, which was a brand-new thing for him. And
this sounds so odd I can hardly believe it myself, but a few
times I would hear him humming a tune as he worked.

Then the first signs of fall appeared, frost came, Papa
stretched his feet on the hearth and kept on spending the
money—only, now there was a real fire which made him
scoot back at times.

"If you gonna do it, why don't you do it and git it over
with?" Mama said.

He looked at her as he would look at a child. "You don't
understand the law. This ain't a criminal case. It's civil. All
right. It'll be tried in November. I'm filing it Saturday. If I
was to a' filed it three months ago, Acroft would a' had all
this time to think up a way around it."

"He won't need much time."

"Jist whose side are you taking in this thing?" he asked.

"Nobody's a tall. Jist one of these days I'll go to Sid
Acroft and I'll ask fer a headstone fer my boy. That's all I'll
ever ask."

He turned to me, as if to say: and you? But he didn't.
Maybe he already knew or maybe he figured he could do it
alone.

I never thought it would really happen. I thought it was
all talk and no do. But one dew-heavy morning, when I had
stayed out of school to pick cotton, a deputy sheriff came
with a summons for me to appear in court on a certain day.

It was done and the deputy was gone before I realized there was really going to be a trial. It is difficult to say now how I felt then. I thought of all the money Papa talked about, and how he would spend it, and how he said Mr. Acroft would never miss it. That night when supper was over and Mama had come back from The House, coughing more than usual, Papa said we'd go to town Thursday and he'd get me new shoes, new shirt, new underwear, new suit: just new everything. Why, we were going to be rich and nearly any merchant in town would credit him with a few clothes. "Hnnnn," Mama said, and coughed and coughed.

The next night Papa changed his mind. If I was to go to the trial all dressed up, he said, then the jury wouldn't feel very sorry for us. They'd think we had plenty.

"He'll have to have a pair of shoes," Mama said.

"You're not in this," he said.

"I don't want no shoes, but he's got to have a pair whether it's a trial or not."

"I know how to handle this," he said. "Let 'em think we're pore as Job's turkey. You know how pore he was?"

"No," Mama said. "And don't care."

"Well, Job's turkey, sister, was so pore he had to lean up against the fence to gobble."

She never laughed. She just coughed for a while.

The trial day came, and I wore my tennis shoes, and I have to say I enjoyed it. It turned out that I was important: I was the one they kept calling back again and again to testify. At first I was a little bit scared, though there were not too many people in the courtroom. It was the jury that got me to thinking. They looked mean. But then, most of them were in overalls and I figured they understood me and my tennis shoes with holes in the toes, and I thought: You're Shardies, too.

Still, I was a little bit afraid of them. When, later, I tried to explain my feeling to Mr. ten Hoor, he made a long speech about justice, or the lack of it, in our county. With much heat he said: "I tell you it is pure accident when justice is accomplished in our courts. Because the world is filled with human beings who are careless with the truth. Don't you ever, ever be a liar. I mean that, even if you have to go hungry and naked and give eyes for an eye and teeth for a tooth. The stupid courts! They begin with stupidity: 'Do you swear to tell the truth, the whole truth and nothing but the truth . . . so help you God?'" Then raising his hand and twisting his face in mockery, he answered himself: "I do. I know you have thus implied that I am a liar by nature. But maybe, with the help of God and the remembrance of my hand on the Holy Bible and the look of honesty in the eyes of all the jurors who never sold a vote and the help of these learned men of the law, who are careful to speak no idle words . . . maybe I will be able to tell the truth and the whole truth, both of them, and also, for good measure, nothing but the truth. O, beasts of the forests, fowls of the air, thank the Holy Creator that you are not like men; you are not lost in a sea of words. . . ."

On and on Mr. ten Hoor went, explaining how a lie was the most useful device in civilization. But to get back to the trial.

I was not thinking about such things, of course, that morning when I first walked into the courtroom. I was thinking about Margo. Would she be there? I hoped so, for only then would she understand how every word would be intended for the absolute truth. I had been warned exactly what to say and what not to say. Warned severely. But I had promised nothing. I was awake some nights before the trial thinking how wonderful it would be to have the money, not all of it, but certainly enough to have a straight foot. And I said to myself: they owe this to me; I could lie and it would not be too bad.

But when the moment came, I told the truth, not because I was afraid of the judge or the jury or the lawyers, nor because I had placed my hand on the Holy Bible and sworn. I told the truth because I had been sitting there for twenty minutes looking at Margo and thinking: she is good and kind and I love her above all beings on the face of this globe. It was that simple. I sat there and I was sick, and I thought the world a very ugly place, not good enough for her.

In the three months since Rudy's death, I had not seen much of Margo. From time to time word would spread that Papa was going to sue the Acrofts, and the story would die

down only to flare again. In times like that you imagine a
million things, and they all seem reasonable and normal: so
it was easy to see her coolness toward me. I would say: you
are one of them, too, Margo; you will devour us, you are an
Acroft. But I never believed a word of it, because something
came over me every time I said her name.

I did manage to treat her with coolness, too, at times; and
right when I thought everything was at its worst, something
new and kind and pleasant would turn up. A word, a look,
a wave of the hand. Maybe you cannot imagine how big a
little thing like that can be in somebody's life. There she
was going to the garden or the smokehouse—I don't remember—and suddenly she waves, and I stand there beside the
barn and think: the world has changed. Oh, but life is made
up of so many little things. I have looked down on Na-
poleon's Tomb and looked up at the Eiffel Tower, and I
have played a game of checkers with a man who to me is
first among all the good men of this world. Ask me now—as
I sit here in this prison recording word after word—ask me
whether I choose the Tomb or the Tower or the checkers.
Yes, life is made up of so many little things that hurt our
hearts and mend them and hurt them over again, and maybe
the thing to remember is: where time is there will be somebody to lift a hand on the way to a garden, or somebody to
sit across the checkerboard, and somebody ready to die because somebody else is not brave, and on and on. And the

small shall be large and the large shall be small. The first shall be last and the last shall be first.

Well, I was grown that morning in the courtroom. I was old, old, and I understood beyond my years. Why, yes, there was Margo and I was in the witness chair for the third time.

The trial was going very well for Papa it seemed to me, when suddenly the question was asked: "Did Sidney Acroft ever once order the child, Rudy, to bridle the mule?"

I said: "He told Vance to."

"Wait a minute now," the lawyer said—Mr. Acroft's lawyer. He was the first man I ever saw wear a tie with the whole picture of a horse spread across it. "Answer the question I asked. Did Sidney Acroft order your brother to bridle the mule?"

"No sir."

"Who did?"

"Papa did."

"But Mr. Acroft didn't?"

"No, he didn't."

He brought me back two more times and had me say the same thing. And from the way Papa and Luke Shakelford looked, I might as well have poured a can of coal oil on twenty thousand dollar bills and struck a match.

When the trial was over, Luke Shakelford more or less jerked me out of the courtroom into his car parked behind court square. On the way home he drove at breakneck speed and kept punching Papa on the shoulder and turning around to look at me and say, "I had a beautiful case! A *beau*tiful case! And you little whipper-snapper . . . I told you what to say. . . . I *told* you! If I was your daddy I'd just beat the living hell out of you. When you've got it all in your hands, right there in your hands, and some little upstart comes along and deliberately slaps it into the wind, for pure mean-ness . . . why, why, blast it all, you knew what you were doing. . . . "

"I told the truth," I said.

"You told the truth! Bah! Don't make me laugh. Haven't you got sense enough to know the other side would lie their heads off to keep what you ought to get? Now, I don't care for myself. It didn't cost me enough to kick about. But when I work like I did and get everything set up and you kick it over just so you can squeak out like a schoolgirl and say, 'I told the truth,' why . . . why . . . then I know what you ought to get and I hope your daddy gives it to you. Now I don't care. . . ." He kept on. He cared so much he couldn't hush and Papa cared so much he couldn't start a syllable.

We didn't have to tell Mama a word. She looked at us and there was the whole story, for Papa's throat was red all the way down. Minutes went by, it seemed, and not a word passed between us. Then Papa went into the kitchen and brought back his leather strap. "What're you going to do?" Mama said.

"I'm going to beat some of the meanness out of him . . . if I can."

I picked up one of the small sticks of firewood near the hearth. "I don't think you can," I said.

The memory of those minutes is horrible to me, so horrible that I remember only the whole and not the details, as you would remember a hailstorm stripping a field but not each icy pellet. Somewhere within those minutes he said, "All right, all right . . ." and everything was settled.

His castle was captured, his dream was shattered, and it was I who had done it all. I cannot deny it. It is a terrible thing to shatter a man's dream. I know that now, and maybe I knew it then. Maybe I knew that a dream is a dream, whether it is a child with a toy or a man with a railroad.

And maybe, too, it goes back beyond me, to other times and other places, and other people whom I have never known, and back, back to the great design of things.

So he packed his clothes in a pasteboard suitcase and as he went out the door he paused long enough to say, "You club-footed fool." Oh, he has forgotten, and I have forgotten—in a way—and the time will come when the world will forget both of us. Why would I put it all down? Because it mattered, I suppose. And maybe because I promised to tell the truth.

I said to Mama, "Is he really gone?"

She shook her head in a way to tell me nothing. She was not one to cry, but there were tears in her eyes. "There was a time," she said, and her hands ran over her apron like a smoothing iron. "There was a time when I thought he was a prince."

6

FROM the day the lawsuit was first mentioned, I lived in dread of the time when Mr. Acroft would tell us we had to move. There was no question: a landlord couldn't keep a sharecropper who had sued him. Therefore, we would soon be jolting on our way with a wagon and team that belonged to some other landlord, somewhere, if we could find him.

Then the trial was over and Papa was gone and I took new hope. I had helped *him*—the landlord—to win, which ought to count for something. Surely he could see the trial hadn't been my fault or Mama's, and the only thing he could hold against me was the fight with Vance. But even that fight had blown over very well, for Vance had been in one summer camp after another in the weeks that followed. Then when fall came, he had been sent to a military school in Missouri (after the manner of the Acrofts and others who had land and money) and he was not at home during the time of the trial.

Now I was the head of the household and I waited to see what Mr. Acroft would do. We had gathered everything except three or four acres of corn. After waiting two days, I went to the barn, took the wagon and team, and began to finish pulling corn. He saw me and told me to put the corn in the feed shed, because the crib was full; and that was all he said. The next day, at the barn, he helped me harness the team and when I started to drive off he said, "Did he really leave?"

"Yessir, I reckon so," I answered.

That was all he asked me.

Then a week passed. The corn was in, but Mr. Acroft had told me nothing. I would have waited longer, but there was nothing left for us to eat. So I had to see Mr. Acroft and find out where we stood. I scrubbed myself all over and put on the best clothes I had and went to his house. It was a raw, windy day, the beginning of December. He had a wonderful fire, and he sat alone beside it, which seemed a great pity to me: so much warmth and only one person. He got up when I entered. He was huge, strong, and there was a trace of worry in his face. I thought: Maybe he is wondering what to do with us. He sat down and told me to sit down, and he sort of looked me over and stretched and yawned, as if to say he never liked sitting around the house. I never sat down. I thought I would get it over with as soon as I could. "I came to see what you're going to do with us."

"Do with you how?"

"I mean, are you going to let us stay on your place?"

"Yes, I'm gonna let you stay."

"I reckon we owe you a whole lot."

"Some folks would say it was a whole lot." There was a

space of silence and he asked, "How much corn was in that piece?"

"Five wagonloads." Then I said, "I want to talk about what we owe you."

He said, "What do you want to talk about it for? You haven't got any money."

I had said the wrong thing, and he had hurt my feelings. I liked him and I hated him, and I said with some anger, "We have to have something to eat, Mr. Acroft!"

He said, "Have you ever been here after anything and failed to get it?"

I swallowed and backed away from the fire, for my face was dripping wet. "When are you going to start the sawmill?"

"In a week or two. Maybe after Christmas."

"Could you give me a job?"

"A job? What about school?"

"I need a job. I don't guess you know it, but Mama's sick. She don't need to be working."

"What's the matter with her?"

"She coughs all the time."

"Maybe she needs some cough syrup."

I don't know what he meant. But whatever it was he made me mad again and I stood there with my chin shaking and the sweat rolling down my face. I would have looked him in the eye and cursed him, except that I was hungry, and when you are hungry you will listen to a great many things and hold your tongue.

After a few seconds, he said, very agreeably, "Did you want to get some things now, Max?"

"Yessir, I did."

By the time he had got the groceries for me I had begun to like him again.

When I got home there was nobody there. I sat down before the fire, dropped my head, and the tears splattered between my feet on the hearth. Why? I don't know. Maybe because I was still too much child though I was almost eighteen years old. Maybe it was because the day was dark and raw. Maybe it was because I knew, even then, that cough syrup would never do Mama any good. In the afternoon I went to see Mr. ten Hoor, whom I had not seen for several days.

It had begun to rain, and I sat beside the window watching isolated drops move back and forth on a clothes line. Mr. ten Hoor was in bed with the old afghan about his shoulders, but he was not the same to me now, and he knew it. Still, I was not exactly grown in his eyes, and there were yet a few things about the world which he knew and I did not know. "What has happened?" he asked.

"Why, nothing." He already knew about the trial and everything that had happened right after it.

"Oh, yes. Something has humiliated your spirit. What is it? The Acrofts?"

"Well, I did get mad at Mr. Acroft this morning, but . . ."

"Exactly. You don't have to tell me. Comes now the time to say: I warned you. I did, lad, in terms far from subtle. So they tramp on you and you go back to be tramped on again. Human nature, I call it. Human nature, it will endure because it hasn't the sense to falter. You went back. . . ."

"I went back because I was hungry, Mr. ten Hoor. That's reason enough for me."

He saw that I was angry and he enjoyed it. I knew he did. I know, too, he was always afraid I would like Mr. Acroft better than I liked him.

"And the Acroft angel? Did you see her this morning?"

So I sat and stared out the window. After a while he said, "Read me some Dickens."

"I don't want to read any Dickens."

"I'm sorry," he said. "I apologize. To lie is bad, to steal is worse, and to humiliate the human spirit is unforgivable. I'm sorry I hurt your feelings. Now will you read?"

"You didn't hurt my feelings. I'm just through with Dickens."

"Through?"

"Yes. Finished. With Dickens and Shakespeare and algebra and poetry—and school. Just through with it, that's all." It was such a dismal day, and the isolated drops looked as though they would freeze on the wire any minute.

I remember his voice, how it came from far off, from years

and years of living: "Listen to me, Max. Bad things have happened, but you're here, you're alive, you're young, you're smart. If ever you put out a flame inside you, it won't burn again. It won't . . . it can't. Today, for the first time, your eyes were dull, lifeless. When you come back to see me again, I want them to be shining the way they were the first time I saw you . . . or else I wish you wouldn't come back . . . for, maybe you understand and maybe you don't . . . but I've tried to give you, to share with you, everything in my mind and heart. Because I . . ."

"I know why, Mr. ten Hoor."

"Yes. Of course, you know. . . ."

The rain increased, beating against the window pane, against the roof. But the sound was peaceful, for we were on the inside and there were no leaks and the room was merely cool, not cold. I could not bring into words what I was thinking: it had to do with the ten Hoor world and the Acroft world. I had gone as far as I could. I had to give up one or the other. Since I could not let go of the Acroft world—groceries and a place to live—there was, then, only one other left to give up. But I could not give it up, either, for whether I saw Mr. ten Hoor or not I remembered London and Plymouth and Paris and Treasure Island and a hundred other places not easily forgotten. Mr. ten Hoor understood those things because he had been there with me, sometimes half asleep with the old afghan about his shoulders, but nevertheless all the way there. When I tried to put this confusion into words, I said, "There's something wrong with the world, Mr. ten Hoor."

"My dear boy, there are many things wrong with the world. But it's not a matter of what's wrong. It's a matter of what you want. Now, what do you really want?"

"I want a house that doesn't leak. A house with good chairs and a good fire. Good clothes and something good to eat. Good land and . . ."

"Oh, hush! Have I taught you nothing? Has your heart shriveled up like a prune. Have the Acrofts ruined you already, with their big white house and thick, green rugs?"

"They *are* green."

"Of course, they are green."

"How did you know? They're new."

"A premonition. Chance. Imagination. And too, the Acrofts are not totally devoid of taste. Oh, I just knew. Don't ask me why. Just tell me why you spieled off that idiotic list when I asked what you wanted. You should want a generous heart, a healthy body, a normal mind. . . ."

"Normal? I wish I was a genius."

"Ah! Ah! So I drag it out. A plow boy wishes to be a genius! You're not. Do you understand that?"

"How do you know what I am?"

"My dear boy, I know more about you than you'll know about yourself for the next ten years. Maybe I ought to tell you, because ten years from now I'll be a part of the earth I came from. I won't be around to help."

"I may not be around to need it."

"An unpleasant observation, but perfectly logical. Were I a fortune teller I would say: life line extremely abbreviated. And then I would give you some abbreviated advice."

"What?"

"Feel. Feel for the cricket on the hearth, the fowls of the air, the beasts, the loved and the unloved. For all things— and you'll be ready to go whether it's thirty-one or ninety-one. And you'll be doing your part against Hitler whether you wear a uniform or not."

When the rain stopped, I left The House and went through the fields and past the barn and waited in the woods lot until the school bus came along the main road. When Margo got off the bus, I called to her and she waited for me. I was muddy halfway to my knees but she seemed not to notice, for she never looked down at me, or so I thought. Still, she said, "Where on earth have you been?"

"I've been talking to Mr. ten Hoor."

"What did that old fogey allow?"

"He allowed that I would die young."

"You probably will. With pneumonia."

We walked on toward the house. She never hurried and she never said a word about school, and she looked as if she knew our meeting was not accidental. I was quiet, because I was wondering if Mr. Acroft was watching us. At the front steps I turned and went around the house. She looked after me for a few seconds and that was all. I felt a tremendous sense of power, and I hoped very much Mr. Acroft had watched us.

That night I dreamed my foot was straight and we lived in a white house, not large, but one well lighted. It was so vivid, so wonderful that I knew, even in dreaming, it could not be true. I wished not to wake, but I awoke with cold slivers of wind crossing my bed. I thought of Mr. ten Hoor and time, and my mind ran something like this: The human mind cannot measure time; it measures action. How long is three minutes? why, three minutes is the length of time it takes to walk with Margo from the road to the front steps.

Was Mr. Acroft looking?

I don't know about that.

Reckon he would care if he *was* looking?

I don't know about that either. They are not totally devoid of taste, Mr. ten Hoor said.

"You git up," Mama said. "I'm not going to call you again."

I got up and we had a good breakfast. I had started off providing very well.

Part Three

I

I WONDER where they are now. Who is living and who is dead? Who fell in the war, and who still spends his days in the woods and goes home at night to shoe-box houses but warm food? I remember their faces and their resin-stained jumpers and their dinner pails and their jokes and their walks and their voices. They are a part of me, like Rudy.

A sawmill gets into your blood: the sound of the hungry saws, the sight of new lumber, the smell of fresh sawdust. More. You are a team, and every man knows. He knows who is good and who is not so good; he knows who likes it and who doesn't care; he knows, without aid of watch or sun, when it's high noon and when it's five; he knows when to joke and when to dry up. He just knows, and if he does not know he does not stay around very long. Mr. Acroft would send him to the timber gang.

You may think it is drudgery to be an off-bearer and carry slabs all day long. That depends. When you have sawmilling in your blood, and the right team around you, off-bearing can be as effortless as a jeweler repairing a watch. You may get

up in the mornings and wonder first thing how many thousands of feet you will cut that day. And if it turns out to be
a record number, you may sing all the way home that night.

But you need a heavy pair of gloves.

I worked barehanded the first week and my hands looked
as if I had tangled with the saw. On Saturday, Mr. Acroft
went to town, and Monday morning he said, "Son, I've got
you a pair of gloves." I never asked him. He just did it. And
that's the way he was. He could be rough, even cruel, but he
took care of his own, and the men loved him. I know because
I was one of them. And for a long time I was not just one,
but the closest one. The men knew that too. Plenty of times
something would come up and the men would say, "Let the
kid tell him," or "Let the kid ask him. He'll do it if the kid
asks him."

I was always The Kid to the men; to Mr. Acroft it was
"Son, this," and "Son, that." But to both I was one of the
team, a fledged member of the crew. Nobody offered to
make things ligher for me or to give me the longest handle,
and that was the best way among men grown old at the
trade.

There was Lee, who had the cleanest-looking face I have
ever seen on a human being. It was smooth, slightly flushed,
immobile, and constantly at attention. He was always solemn,
quiet, and would barely part his lips when somebody told a
man-woman joke that made the others cackle. He did not
care for jokes, did not need them, but they did not bother

him any more than the hum of the saws bothered him. He had a daughter, Margo's age, who played on the high-school basketball team; so I guess he was too old for the war. And Chief Chick-Chick, the sawyer, with his broken leg, who could set a carriage to one-sixteenth of an inch blindfolded. He clucked like a chicken all the time: so many clucks meant turn the log this way boys or that way, and so on. Uncle Bill Bob with his sawdust scoop; Charlie Wash and his twists of home-grown tobacco; the two Negroes who claimed they were twins but were not even brothers; Herman Baker and his herculean trick of lifting a log rather than rolling it; Mr. Daniels who had coal black eyebrows and blue eyes: we called him Daniel-in-the-Lion's-Den. And above all Victor Wells. There was the timber gang but it was not really a part of us.

The war was almost upon us. The price of lumber climbed steadily, until ordinary two-by-fours from buttermilk pine were forty-five dollars a thousand. Mr. Acroft knew when to cash in. He kept the mill going right through crop time, and by the end of that summer I was making two dollars and a half a day: twice what I got in the beginning. That was an awful lot of money to me: fifteen dollars a week. We bought clothes and things to eat and papered two rooms of our house and lived as we had never lived before. Besides, we put a dollar up every week for a tomb for Rudy, and I almost had Mama into the notion to quit working at The House.

One might think off-bearing made me lean. It didn't. I was heavier than I had ever been. After six months, I was brown and I was hard. Nobody at the mill could shake me around except Herman Baker, and he was liable to shake anything. Mr. Acroft would sometimes clamp his hand over my shoulder and say, "You're coming out of the kinks!" That was all right. He only pretended to shake me, and we got along fine.

We rode to the mill together every morning just about daybreak—he on his white stallion, I on one of his bay mares. That was what he loved: early morning, day breaking, new smoke on the air, a chorus of invisible birds, and the screak of our saddles. He was one man then, and coming home at night he was another man, dark, brooding, irritable, distant—except when Margo would meet us, and then he would change quickly as a child into his early-morning mood. He would get down and walk with her the rest of the way back to the house or the barn. If they asked me, I would get down and walk too. When we walked together, with her between us, I would go home so full of the goodness of the world that I could not go to sleep until way past my usual time. More. When that happened I would always get up an hour earlier the next morning and I would hurry to the barn and have the horses saddled and waiting when Mr. Acroft got there. He would grin and kid me about something or other, and I would know he was not blind nor entirely cool toward what was going on in my world. Oh, he could be splendid: like buying you a Thermos bottle for coffee on cold days and saying, "Here it is," in such a way you would know he expected nothing in return. A trifle, of course, but Mr. ten Hoor used to say a rich man's wealth is made up of pennies and a good man's deeds are made up of little mercies and sacrifices and considerations. Still, there were things about Mr. Acroft that Mr. ten Hoor didn't know, and I guess he didn't know anything about Victor Wells.

Victor was tall and lean, weather darkened, and as strong as any man needed to be. His dark, steady eyes reflected a whole world of peacefulness; and his slow, pleasant way of speaking was an indication that his world would not change. From the first time I saw him in his overalls and jumper and long-billed cap, something in me bowed down. I think I knew even in the beginning that he was something apart, good, honest, and the kind of man you go looking for when the world is dark. I had no idea he would cause the first open trouble between me and Mr. Acroft.

It was understood that Victor Wells could get along with anybody, but it was further understood that nobody pushed him around. I had been working at the mill several weeks when I heard the story of the quilting frames. Victor had had four frames cut for his wife and had carried them home and left them on his front porch to dry. A few days later, Earl Baker had had a set of frames cut and for some reason left them at the mill. That night they were stolen. On the following Sunday, Earl happened to pass Victor's house and he happened to see the set of frames. Monday morning, at the mill, Earl wanted to know when Victor was going to bring his frames back. A joke was a joke, he said, but the business had gone far enough. When Victor claimed the frames as his own, Earl promptly called him a liar. Even more promptly, Victor raised the claw hammer in his hand and knocked Earl in the head.

When the dust of that matter settled, Mr. Acroft sent Earl Baker to the timber gang, which was his way of saying Victor was right and Earl was wrong. Because it was Mr. Acroft's policy to send any man who got out of line to the timber gang; he considered it a severe punishment.

I supposed that Mr. Acroft and Victor got along all right together, because I would often hear Mr. Acroft asking Victor's advice about something. And it was the two of them, together, who got up the fishing trip. Victor had the name of being the best grappler around. But once or twice when something was said about it, Mr. Acroft would let it be known that he was a pretty good grappler too.

We went fishing late one Saturday afternoon, all of the mill gang and a few of the timber gang. Mr. Harmon carried us in his school bus to Box Ridge and there we set out on foot to a section of the river known as Willow Bend. Victor was in a high humor and so was most everybody else. Somebody kept saying, "Don't worry about gettin' lost. Victor knows the way. He was practickly raised down here."

It was a standing joke. Now and then some man would ask, "Say you was practickly raised down here, Vic?"

I never knew whether the joke had a special meaning because Victor and his daddy and his granddaddy had lived on Willow Bend all their lives; or whether it was the men's way of putting Victor ahead of Mr. Acroft, once we were away from the sawmill. But Victor had obviously become the new leader, and Mr. Acroft was taking full notice. It seemed to me that everybody was taking full notice except Victor, who had nothing on his mind but catching fish.

We came to the place where the grappling would begin and in no time at all Victor had pulled a four-pound catfish from beneath an old stump. Within a few minutes he had another larger than the one before. So the men waded around Victor, and left Mr. Acroft all by himself. I went back to be with Mr. Acroft because I halfway felt sorry for him, and I was hoping he would come up with a big one. He finally got hold of a channel cat the size to make you wonder whether to keep it or whether to throw it back. But his disappointment was lessened by the fact that the men had suddenly scattered away from Victor, as if they had learned their lesson and were ready to succeed on their own. Mr. Acroft dropped his fish back into the water and started all over again.

"You stay with me," Mr. Acroft said, "and we'll come up with a prize." He started for a shady spot where the holes in the bank looked likely. I followed. We were directly across the stream from Victor. By then all the other men were a hundred yards downstream, as if they must keep ahead of Victor if they expected to catch anything. Mr. Acroft worked the holes slowly and carefully, running his arm into the crevices, or sometimes shoving his body into the cracks until only his head and shoulders stuck out, while his feet kicked around exploring every corner where a big cat could be hiding.

Mr. Acroft was jammed into a hole, exploring with his feet, when I heard Victor call. Or rather, I heard, "Come 'ere! Come 'ere!" Which was little more than a whisper. I doubt that Mr. Acroft even heard.

I went running in the waist-deep water toward Victor, who quickly showed me where to get and what to do. I held to an old stump with both hands and shoved my feet past the stump into the river bank, and my heart hammered because I was actually afraid. All I could think of was a monstrous snake coiled in the dark hole, but Victor was telling me what to do and so I had to do it. He kept whispering, "Easy now . . . easy now . . . he'll come out." Then there was a great heave and something slapped my shins and I jerked back as if a snake had actually struck me. I felt a sharp pain near my left ankle.

There was Victor struggling to keep his feet while the biggest channel cat I had ever seen seemed to have swallowed his arm. I was yelling, "You got him! You got him!" And Mr. Acroft, jammed into the other bank, across the river, with only his head and shoulders showing, unable to look our way, was yelling, "Max! Max! Where the hell are you? He's coming out!"

I rushed back across the stream, faintly aware of the pain around my left ankle, and I reached Mr. Acroft just as a huge channel cat—which seemed even larger than Victor's—splashed out of the hole where I should have been and went free into the stream. By then Mr. Acroft had pulled back enough to look around at me and past me where Victor was landing his prize.

He opened his mouth and I waited for a string of curses. But instead, he closed his lips slowly and turned redder and redder and the sweat popped out even on his ears.

"Damn you," he said, hardly loud enough for Victor to hear. "Who the hell are you with anyway?"

Victor had got out of the water and was going downstream toward the men. We looked after him.

"That's a shame," Mr. Acroft said.

"What?" I asked.

"That you'd run off right when I get one hemmed. It was a damn sight bigger than the one he got."

I was feeling low and wishing I hadn't come at all, or wishing I had stayed with Victor. I felt the pain around my ankle. I looked away from Mr. Acroft and wouldn't answer. I got out of the water and sat on the bank and watched the blood run off my foot into the sand. I knew what had happened: in jerking backward I had snagged my foot on the stump root. It was an ugly gash.

Mr. Acroft looked at the blood and said, "Did Victor's fish get you?"

I never answered him.

"If you'd been over here that wouldn't have happened," he said.

I searched my soggy pockets for a handkerchief, but I had lost it in the water or else I had never brought one. Mr. Acroft knew what I was looking for, because he took out his own handkerchief and wrung the water out; and I knew he was about to offer it to me. Then he called to Victor, who stopped and turned. "Don't have this boy stick his foot in no more holes."

Victor looked puzzled for a second, then went on without a word.

"What do you care?" I said. "You're not worried about my foot." I got up and started downstream toward Victor.

Mr. Acroft climbed out and followed me.

"Do you want this handkerchief?" he said.

"No," I said.

When we reached Victor, the men had surrounded him, looking at the fish; and he was telling how the two of us had got it. For half a second I thought I would ask Victor for his handkerchief and sit down before Mr. Acroft and tie up my foot. But I thought better of it: I knew I might have gone too far already.

Something had gone too far. Because on Monday morning Mr. Acroft sent Victor to the timber gang. He told Victor the men were not getting the logs in fast enough and he wanted him to straighten them out. He had a point, for the logs did come in too slow. But I knew there was more to it than that, and when the time came I told Mr. Acroft so.

But first, I acted cool to him. From the minute I knew he had sent Victor to the timber gang I started a war of silence. I spoke when I was spoken to and that was all. And if anything would get Mr. Acroft, it was silence, especially around the barn or on the way to work or at the mill. I really thought it would get him before it did, and there were times when I thought I might not hold out. But I would think of Victor, who was as good a hand as a man could ever hope to have, shoved off on the timber gang where the work was harder, more dangerous, and more aggravating. For what? For being a better fisherman, I supposed.

On the fourth morning Mr. Acroft broke out with a sudden explosion. "I've had enough of this! What the hell is eating you?"

"What's eating you?" I answered. "You didn't have to send Victor to the timber gang."

He kept his great eyes on me and it was all I could do not to melt beneath his authority. "By god, I'll put my men where I want to put them. And they'll stay there too."

"Sure," I said. "Because he's got three kids and a wife to

feed. He'll stay there. But not because he's afraid of you. He's not afraid of anybody."

There was a sort of cold twitching around his mouth. "Do you think you mean enough to me to make me bring him back to the mill?"

I answered, "I don't think I mean enough to you to make you do anything."

The war of silence went on the rest of that day and all day Friday and Saturday.

Monday morning Victor was back at the mill. So the world seemed right again, the war was over, and there was something new in Mr. Acroft's face. As Mr. ten Hoor put it: What is chance and what is an answer? Mr. Acroft grew old in that one week. I loved him and I hated him and I suppose I was both right and wrong.

But anyway, the world was all right for a while.

2

ON A wonderful September morning, after Margo had met us and walked with us the night before, I got up early—according to my way—and had the horses ready when Mr. Acroft came to the barn. He was in a lively humor, and he made some kind of joke about his way with the women when he was young, and asked me what I would say if a woman said thus and so to me. It was the kind of vulgar talk that does not seem vulgar when it comes from men like him. I mention it because at those times he seemed closest to me. It was not really good daylight when we left the barn, but before we reached the woods we could distinguish the vast sweep of colors coming chiefly from the hickory and oak and gum. He kept on, the best ever, teasing and joking and asking serious questions about how much timber there would be in such and such a spot. The men always said, "Ask him anything between daybreak and sun-up and you'll git it." Which was about right. As we crossed the hillside overlooking the mill, he reined the stallion to a halt and more or less surveyed everything in sight, all of which was his.

"What would you do if you owned it?" he asked.

It startled me, and sounded very much like, "What would you do if you were King?" If I did not wonder then I wonder now what he was doing? Was he being perverse with someone practically penniless? Was he trying to tell me that he understood Margo and me, that he too, had been young once? Or was it just a chance question, the kind he would have asked Herman or Uncle Bill Bob, and now was asking me, as a man, not as a boy eighteen and one-half years old. I am thinking back, wondering, as we all wonder about the past. But there I have to stop, for I never had a chance to answer his question.

A cry came at us like a deadly arrow, came from the sawmill and struck us cold. It was so inhuman and inappropriate

for that hour of the morning, so weighted with the super-
natural that I shivered with fear, and I know it unsettled Mr.
Acroft too. He looked shaken and said, "What you reckon
that is?" At that moment we made out the words, "Oh,
God!"

"It's somebody!" he said.

We broke toward the mill at the same time, and he beat
me there by a length or two. A man lay face down in the bark
and sawdust and splinters and his knee was crushed under an
enormous cypress log. At first glance I did not recognize the
man, which, of course, was because I was excited and because
he lay as he did. Now at such times you are liable to do and
say the most uncalled-for things. And the first thing I said
was, "Who is it?"

Mr. Acroft said, "What the hell does that matter?"

So I grabbed a heavy slab and he grabbed it too and we
prized the end of the log around until the man was free. It
was Victor. Again I was shocked, because his shoulders
looked so narrow now and there seemed to be not one pulse
beat of strength left in him. His eyes were closed. I suppose
he had fainted.

Mr. Acroft must have known what a job it is to handle an
almost lifeless two-hundred-pound man. In any case, I will
say that he used his head. Maybe we could have got Victor
on the stallion or the mare and carried him, and maybe we
couldn't have. It is one thing to think about and quite an-

other thing where there is real sawdust, real resin and real fences to get through if you are carrying him to the nearest car or truck.

The thing to do was to get him to Mr. Harmon's school-bus. There were not many choices as to how. There were fences and hedge rows and creeks, and even if one of the log wagons had been there, that minute, it would have been of little use. We had to carry him, and we knew it right away. It seems to me it didn't take Mr. Acroft two minutes to make a stretcher with a piece of tarpaulin and two poles. We started off fine, and he was not so heavy in the beginning.

There was not much question of what had happened: he had simply got to the mill early, as he often did, and had started rolling logs down the skids and had probably slipped or tripped over something. But I wondered, as we went along and he got heavier and heavier, why it had happened to the best and most reliable man in the crew.

When I thought I couldn't go another ten steps, I gathered new strength somehow and went on. I thought: this man is dying and I am well. I have to do it. Maybe it was a tremendous effort to prove myself worthy of having been spared the fate of Victor. Later, during the war, I had similar experiences in the face of death. But in every case, that synthetic strength lasted only for a little while. So at last I stumbled. Victor groaned, and Mr. Acroft, breathing hard, said, "What's the matter?" He was in his dark mood.

We were going up a steep, rocky hillside. My arms ached and my knees buckled and caught and buckled again. My left foot hit a rock. I stumbled to my knees, and rose again at the sound of Mr. Acroft's voice, harsh and tense, "What's the matter?"

Blood now was rolling down the canvas and dripping off the lower end. I turned queasy at the sight, for the thought of pain is often more terrible to me than the pain itself. The vines and briars and rocks were too much for my left foot again. I stumbled to my knees. Mr. Acroft cursed and added, angrily, "If you'd left him where I put him this wouldn't have happened."

"I didn't bring him back," I said. But the thought that I really had brought him back from the timber gang put new strength in me.

We had almost reached the top of the hill and from there we would be able to see Mr. Harmon's house. But the false step came again; a vine, a rock, I don't know. This time I fell and my end of the stretcher crashed and Victor dropped off the canvas. Mr. Acroft wheeled. He cursed as if the world were against us—no, him—and he said, "Can't you stand up?"

I had dropped my end of the stretcher. I was not thinking of Victor Wells. If he died, he just died. I said, "Can't you act like a human being? I might do better if I had two good feet."

He stared at me, completely shaken, because people did

not usually talk back to him. There was in his eyes the frosty glare of annihilation. I was actually afraid of him. I still wonder sometimes what he might have done if Victor had not come out of his coma long enough to say, "Where am I?"

We were quickly together again, aware of death and our mission. Silently we went back to the business before us, and when I stumbled, once again, just before we reached the Harmon house, Mr. Acroft did not say anything. He even pretended not to notice.

Then he got Mr. Harmon in a hurry and after we had loaded the stretcher in the bus, he motioned that I was to go with them. From time to time he said something to Mr. Harmon, directing or explaining. The road was winding and rough. I took off my jumper and put it under Victor's head. Mr. Acroft saw, and maybe he nodded his approval, but he never said anything to me. A mile or so later he took off his own leather jacket and I put it under Victor's head. This, too, without a word.

We got there and we got him inside, and I knew only that he was not dead yet. The smell of the hospital worried me. I went outside and sat on the curb, and wondered if Mr. Acroft would have any trouble finding me if I should be needed.

Sometime after sun-up Mr. Harmon came out and said Victor was doing fine. He also said that Mr. Acroft wanted me inside. I remember the sunlight and the long shadows and the smell of gasoline when Mr. Harmon's bus moved into the street and away. Then the hour that followed is so strange I can hardly account for it, and so simple I can hardly relate it. Within a matter of minutes I was in a small room, lying on a high narrow table, staring up at the light and the largest fan I had ever seen. On one side of me was a doctor and on the other side was Mr. Acroft. The doctor began to probe around on my foot while I lay thinking about the holes in my socks. Oh, I thought of a hundred other things too. I thought of Jesus and the lame, and I was full of faith: I thought, Yes, He did, I will never doubt it again. My heart beat fast and I could feel the sweatdrops go down my face like crawling ants.

I never asked anything. Why should I have asked anything? I was too afraid one syllable from me might break the spell. And besides, I was in a dream, in a state of shock, and I did not really know what was happening. I thought: When I see her and she looks on my foot, straight and whole . . . I could not think beyond that. My heart was in such a wild state that I supposed the doctor was thinking: Why, this boy couldn't stand an operation; it would scare him to death. I prayed for strength to answer, for strength not to tremble. But I remained dumb and I kept on trembling. I could hardly feel the probing of my foot.

Then the two went out. I lay there staring, listening, waiting, and hoping to the edge of my being, while the world grew colder and colder. At such times you may hear a hound bark that you heard years ago, or the wail of a train whistle that belonged to your childhood; or over your closed eyelids (for I had closed mine to shut out the world) there may pass the face of somebody you loved, or there may appear the image of something alone, man or animal. And it seems that you have forgotten what life was like, only to wake and remember, and you know that to live—whole and sound—is the best of all good things. And you know because you have never had any proof, which is the best way of all knowing.

They were gone for a long time, and the time was both terrible and wonderful. Outside I burned with the fever of doubt, and inside I bubbled with the cool spring of hope, thinking: I have waited all my life for this and at last it is here, unexpected, alarmingly sudden. I cannot describe my feeling of happiness, but in the midst of it I was struck with that insidious animal of sadness who raised its ugly head and crowded my memory: I recalled a Saturday morning of the year we lived on the Benjamin place; Mama, heavy with Rudy, standing in the kitchen doorway watching Papa go off to town to get drunk; she was saying, "Now, are you going to come back *like that* or not? Because you know it's my time and I don't know what the consequences would be if I was to be here by myself." It was the word *consequences* that got me. It was the biggest word I ever heard her use, and I had already learned to use it by the time he came home that night drunk.

I sat up on the table and opened my eyes wide to drive away the unhappy image of that day on the Benjamin place.

I fastened my gaze on the shining instruments in the cabinet before me. Hope came bubbling again, slowly. When I heard steps, I lay down, for that was the way they had left me.

The doctor was alone. Until then I had paid very little attention to the doctor's features. He was a middle-aged man with plenty of gray hair, too gray for his years, slightly stooped shoulders, a short, rocking walk that matched his staccato speech, and blue eyes of the depth and color that one trusts. He asked me how old I was and I said I was eighteen, would be nineteen in February. He shook his head and was about to say something to me when Mr. Acroft came back into the room. So he turned toward the door and said, "Bone heals so much faster before you're eighteen."

Mr. Acroft nodded as if he agreed or already knew.

The doctor placed my foot flat on the table and pulled a machine around so that the mysterious arm of it was merely six inches away from my ankle. In my excitement I could not remain still, for I thought the operation had commenced. The doctor said, "Hold still. I just want a picture, that's all."

Mr. Acroft laughed.

I didn't say a word, of course, but I thought the picture business was silly. If my foot was ever straight I didn't want anything around to remind me of when it was crooked. I supposed he wanted it as a matter of record, to show what a wonderful doctor he was. That reminded me of how much it might cost, and it made me shiver. But I didn't care. If it took ten years to pay for it, why that was a mere nothing.

The doctor left the room, and a minute later I was led down the hall to room seventeen. Mr. Acroft did not follow me. He was gone for an hour or more, and when he returned he had new underwear and pajamas for me. For a long time afterward I thought of pajamas as something you wore only in a hospital. But the thing to remember: he got them and he got them without my asking.

I was to remain quietly in bed; I was to have liquids and mashed potatoes and toast; I was to go to sleep as early as possible. The great event would occur the next morning at nine o'clock.

I recall vividly that wonderful, terrible, restless day. I was anything but quiet, and my mind must have covered a million uninterrupted miles. Mr. Acroft went home and returned after supper. He told me he had seen Mama, who said she wasn't worried; and he told me Margo said, "Cheerio." Then he left because he said I had to go to sleep early.

Sleep, indeed! Sleep on the night before you are to have the highest thing you have ever hoped for? And Margo said, *Cheerio.* Just a word to somebody else. But to me . . . Well, *life* is just a word, and *death* is just a word, and *cheerio* was more than both of them.

The nurse expected me to go to sleep. Eight o'clock, nine o'clock, eleven . . . The door came back ever so softly. She whispered, "Why don't you go to sleep?"

"I'm trying."

"Need more cover?"

"No, ma'am."

"I'd better give you another tablet. You know you've got to sleep."

"Yes, ma'am."

Midnight and one and maybe others. But somewhere along there I went to sleep. And I dreamed that I woke up crying and holding my foot, because I liked myself fairly well as I was.

Maybe it wasn't altogether a dream, for a few hours later, with the waves of ether passing over me as I counted slowly, I had a horrible, sinking feeling, and I cried out, "Stop! Stop! I like myself all right!" Even now I am beyond words to express the fear that went through me as I rose on wings of ether.

3

THE PAIN was great. The seven days and nights of that first week were one solid flame, consuming everything except the fire itself. And my constant thought was, "Why didn't they leave me alone?" The price, it seemed, was much too high, and if I could have undone the cast which kept my toes pointing upward instead of flopping over to the right, I would have undone it.

"Listen, Max!" Sometimes the nurse would give me a light

slap on the face. She would explain why the ache in my bone was so intense, why the fire was constant, why I could not have a pill or a shot. I refused to listen; I believed they had not done their work well, and I said so.

The week passed as one section of time undivided by light and darkness, undivided by anything except the one brief visit of Margo. I never really knew when she came or when she went; and whatever she said I have long since forgotten. But I am certain I asked her please not to come back again. And that was how the first week went.

On the eighth day there was a vast change, such a change that I began to hope I would live. Mama came to see me that day, and she was happier than I had ever seen her. Not then, but later, I tried to imagine what she must have felt. She would not sit down and she would hardly take her eyes from the foot of my bed and the cast. With the two of us alone, she whispered she would have come earlier but she was waiting for Mrs. Halterbin to make her a new print dress. I understood perfectly, because we are like that. She asked if the dress was all right, which really meant: Was her entire appearance all right? When I laughed, I knew she was reassured not only about herself but also about me. We talked for a long time about things that mattered and things that didn't matter. When she was gone and the day was over, I began to believe again in the good things of the world.

As the pain gradually left me, my hopes gradually soared again: the hope of all the intangibles which afford a certain

peace of mind. Too, the definite hope of a new-formed
foot—I began to wonder how a shoe was going to feel.
Everything was running at high tide, until I got to thinking
why Margo had not come back to see me. It was time for new
considerations, time to look into the future with changed
ideas—and a changed body. Maybe I was to be a new person.

It was also time to wonder why I had been put into the
hospital in the first place. I wondered about it—so I
thought—from every angle possible. In the morning, in the
afternoon, or at midnight, I seemed always to arrive at one
clear conclusion: Mr. Acroft had done this thing for Margo,
first; for me, second.

That being true, what did I think of it?

Well, it might take several weeks to reach the answer. In
the meantime, I would neither like nor dislike what had
happened. From one angle, I would have to be on Mr.
Acroft's side. He knew our world—mine and Margo's—and
he knew or thought there was this strange thing between us,
a thing which he could remedy. And he had set about his
plan to remedy, without questions or explanations. And
wasn't that really the best and kindest way? What more
could I ask of him?

There was the possibility that he had done this thing for
me, first, which was a pleasant thought. I had been helpful,
usually agreeable, and devoted; I had bowed to his judg-
ments; I had given him my fullest measure of time and

energy and thought. There were lots of things I could do which none of the older hands could do. All of this he knew.

Again, there was the possibility (thinking of Mr. ten Hoor) that he had done this thing in the same spirit he would have his stallion shod: simply a thing that should be done. But such thinking was too unpleasant. And I had already been sobered and staggered with the knowledge that my hospital and doctor bill would total something like one thousand dollars. That was a lifetime of work to me. There was finally nothing for me but to crawl back into the dim hole of ignorance and say these things are too heavy for my mind.

So the second week ended with Mama coming back again. This time she brought the money which we had saved for Rudy's tombstone.

She also brought a book from Mr. ten Hoor, and a note saying he hoped I would be well soon and so on and he had fifty dollars which he wanted me to have because he knew what the expenses would be like. That got me to thinking about the money again, and I decided it was time I said something to Mr. Acroft, for one of the nurses had said I would be going home in a couple of weeks.

My chance came. Mr. Acroft was alone with me, and I put it to him straight. "How am I ever going to pay for all this?" I asked.

"You're not," he said. He was sitting in a straight-back chair with his legs crossed, and a cigar to keep him occupied. The smoke floated around his eyes but it seemed not to bother him.

"I know I can't right now. But I'm going to pay you sometime."

"I'm not paying for it either," he said, then waited for me to be surprised.

"Then who is?"

"I'll explain later."

He left me with the mystery which was to remain a mystery for the next four days. In the meantime, I imagined a great many things and wondered who else on earth could be concerned with me. I would have suspected Mr. ten Hoor, but his note and offer of help ruled him out. Besides, I was certain that fifty dollars was all he had in the world. There was Margo, of course, but I could not stand to think she was behind any of it. Another thing too: Mr. Acroft could be joking me. Whatever I thought, I always ended in a sweating state with damp spots on the sheet and pillow case. And I would have blue hours when I wished this thing had not been started. So far as I could tell at that time I liked my life better the way it had been.

Then the time came for Mr. Acroft to tell me. I was sitting up in bed and had just finished the noon meal. Mr. Acroft came in but he did not sit down. For five or ten minutes he walked nervously about the room. I noticed and knew something was about to happen. He was neither in his bright daybreak mood nor in his dark sundown mood; he was somewhere in between, on unfamiliar ground. "Max, I wanted to talk to you about the doctor bill and the hospital bill."

I waited, not knowing what I was supposed to say. It had all been so strange, anyway: particularly the suddenness of everything.

"It's a whole lot, you know."

I nodded.

"I'm going to tell you how I want to handle it."

But he didn't tell me for a few minutes. I give him full credit for that. He moved about the room and sat down and maybe he said something about something else and finally got up again. "I've got insurance on all the mill hands, you know. Now Victor's bill won't be much. I'm going to pay that. And we'll put the insurance on you, like you got hurt."

I just felt myself turn pale, because I was afraid . . . afraid. . . . I must have known in an instant that I would have to go through with it, and that some day it would catch up with me. And if I think on it long enough even now I get sick, because that same fear comes back to me. I was caught and doomed and there is both the beginning and the end; and you and I and all of us can cry *why* until the echoes echo, but what earthly good? I remember myself slumping down in the bed and I remember how afraid I was. I also remember, somewhere in that time, my voice like another person's voice saying: "Mr. Acroft, I know I'm a Harper and a Shardy. I know my daddy would tell anything, and steal and do most anything. But why did you do this to me?"

He just kept the steel of his eyes on me, and I said, "I'll pay you, Mr. Acroft. I'll pay you if it takes all my life. If Victor ever found out . . ."

He said, "Do you know how much a thousand dollars is? All you have to do is sign some papers."

"What about Victor?" I asked.

"He won't know. Nobody will know except me and you and the insurance man. I've already talked to him. He'll fix it."

"Why would he fix it?"

"Because he'd rather pay a thousand dollars for you than three or four thousand dollars' damages if Victor decided to sue."

"What if Victor did want to sue?"

"Don't you know he's not the kind of man for that? But if he did . . . well, if he did I'd fix it someway."

The hospital smell was so close on me that I was sick. I closed my eyes. I thought of Victor on his crutches, the way he had looked when he came by to see me. I wanted to sink or to rise, anything to free me of that room and the hospital smell and the image of Victor limping.

"Are you going to help me?" he asked.

"Yes," I answered.

"And do what I say?"

"Yes."

4

I WAS glad to get home, though I was left in the house by myself most of the time. After a few days I could walk from one room to another and after two weeks I was going almost wherever I wanted to go.

The money we had saved for Rudy's tombstone was finally spent for a steel brace, which was necessary after the cast was taken off. (I never accepted Mr. ten Hoor's offer to help.) In the mornings I would get up early and make my own breakfast—for Mama was gone—and then I would piddle about the house until noon. I remember the time well because I wondered a lot about people who never have anything to do. They get up and go with the wind, and how they could be happy I cannot understand.

In the afternoon I would go sit on the hillside and watch the cotton pickers. There was not much cotton that year, for Mr. Acroft had taken so many hands away from the fields to the sawmill. As I watched the pickers, I would grow impatient, and finally my whole body would ache faintly with the desire to be well and in the midst of the pickers.

Margo would come to see me at ten minutes to four. The time would vary no more than three or four minutes from day to day. At first she came to bring small things which I might need, and later, when I seemed to need nothing, she still came.

We would go down to the four springs, which flowed freely even in that dry autumn, and I would think time and again: she is going to ask me who paid the hospital bill. And I would think about what we had done—Mr. Acroft and I— and she would notice. Her eyes would be filled with questions at times and at other times it seemed that she knew all about the insurance and every other thing worth knowing.

"Why are you so far off?" she would ask.

I would answer that I was not far off, though actually I would be in the hospital room signing the papers again, or hearing Mr. Acroft when he told me what I must do, or seeing the limping figure of Victor.

"You have changed," she would say.

"I haven't."

"Oh, yes . . . you've changed."

Then one day I saw she had changed too. Her hair was combed straight back and her face looked longer and thinner, and she seemed much older and quieter. I remember I had the impression that she was living the future too intensely, just as old people sometimes live the past. In a vague way, I said something about her living in the future.

"You certainly don't," she accused. "You never promise me anything."

"What could I promise you?" I asked. "I haven't got anything to promise."

"Now you see? You see, don't you?" Tears filled her eyes and she got up and ran off.

It was several days before she came back again. By the second or third day I thought I had been mistreated and I was angry. But still I went every day to the same spot among the pines above the springs and waited. Then one day when I saw her coming I thought my body would rise against my will and rush toward her. She sat down beside me and I think it was a long time before even our fingers touched or a word was spoken. Then we began to talk and it was like reclimbing a mountain which has been climbed long enough ago for you to forget the way. At last we reached the top of our talk and a heavy silence fell between us. I felt as if we had started at the beginning and reached the end, and I waited uneasily for what would come next.

I watched Margo closely. She sat with her hands flat on the pine needles, her back straight, her head tilted forward a little. For the first time I thought of her as being beautiful; until then, I suppose I had never cared whether she was or wasn't. She moved forward and placed her hand over my ankle and the bandage. Without looking at me, she said, "I wish Papa hadn't done it."

"Why?" I said.

"Because I liked you the way you were."

I watched her closely but I could not see all of her face. But I could see enough that it reminded me of watching her feed a crippled pigeon. I knew she had thought more of that pigeon than all the others; but when it was well, she had given it away. I was suddenly weak. I lay back and breathed deeply.

She did not move. She said, "You're almost well. In a little while you'll go off somewhere. You'll never stay here." Tears fell on her face.

I closed my eyes. I wanted to tell her of the million things I suddenly remembered: the Hunter place, and the autumn pears, which in September began to ripen and fall. We would come from the cotton fields, hungry and thirsty, and pass by the trees as if they were not there, because every pear was forbidden to us though they fell one by one or by the dozens when the wind was high and lay on the ground and rotted— all but three or four which stayed and stayed until finally, in the dead of winter, they looked like dried prunes tied among the bare branches. And every morning except Sunday, Mr. Hunter would leave his house and open his store at the crossroads and sit on a nail keg and wait and softly chew his tongue just as he did in church when the preacher was loud and strong; and at noon he would eat cheese and crackers but before eating he would fall on his knees and say, "Our Fodder in Heaven, we thank Thee for all Thy blessings. Help us to be kind and generous, our Fodder. Help us to turn Thy way and sin no more. . . ." And the pears fell and lay where they fell. Rudy could say "our Fodder" just like old man Hunter.

I remembered that and more, and how the pain around my

ankle for those first few days had made me sick at my stomach. I opened my eyes. I saw her take her hand from my foot.

"Do you love me?" she said.

"Yes," I answered. "I love you more than anybody in the world . . . that's all I can promise. And I wish . . . I wish I'd never got well. . . ."

She put her fingers over my lips. Her hair fell around my face and it smelled like spring water in April woods, when all the world is alive and singing.

My mind was leaping with every pulse beat: somewhere at the mill Mr. Acroft stood in his dark mood; somewhere at the mill Victor limped in the dry afternoon sunlight. My hand trembled as it did when I signed the lie that a log had rolled on me—not Victor.

She pushed at my forehead as if to open my eyes, to find the secret. But I did not open my eyes and I did not say anything. I remembered her hands on the pigeon she had healed and given away.

5

THE FIRST week of December I went back to the sawmill. I still limped and was not well enough to begin off-bearing, but there were light jobs which seemed exactly fitted for me. It seemed that nothing had changed, and yet I knew well enough the old way was gone.

There was Victor, limping still, and I thought: I must stay away from him; if it had been anybody but him it would not be so bad. But there he was stronger than before, more above us than ever, not bothering to notice our little tricks. He was like a god, even with the limp and his overalls; and I wondered what hour he would say, "Go on and mind your own business. I know all about it."

I tried to stay away from him. But it was no good. I was drawn to him as a moth to a strong light, and there I stayed and was singed again and again, whenever he said a word or gave me a look, and especially when he joked me about something.

Mr. Acroft saw it, and I knew he saw it, but he acted as if nothing had changed. Still, I felt I had lost him. Our morning rides were no longer the same; his bright daylight mood had vanished, and nothing, not even the dark mood, had filled the void. I rode along beside him, remembering what he had done, for me, for Margo, for himself; I remembered and felt small inside and did not wish to watch him as I once had. I am sure he rode along and remembered too. It was at least some comfort then that Victor did not know the dark secret.

But I am certain, almost beyond doubt, that in time Mr. Acroft and I would have come together again, though we might never have reached that understanding which existed in the time of our innocence.

The war came upon us like Victor's accident. We went back to work Monday morning wondering what the meaning could be. Maybe I thought it was not really so, or maybe I thought it was something far off which would be finished in a few weeks, something hardly to be heard above the grind of the sawmill. And if I saw smoke and flame, quick blood and torn flesh, at least I never felt such blood and flesh would ever be mine. I asked Mr. Acroft what was going to happen. He answered, almost in the old way, "Why, I don't know, son."

In a day or two I understood from Margo that Mr. Acroft had telephoned Vance to come home at once. In another day or two Vance was there.

I suppose he had heard something about my foot, for he did not seem surprised when we came face to face the afternoon he got home. He was coming out of the alley of the barn when I rode up on the white stallion, which, so far as I knew, was still forbidden to him. There I sat on the white stallion (Mr. Acroft had come home early on the mare) with my left foot straight in the stirrup and Vance taken by envy and anger. I dismounted, unsaddled, and stabled the stallion before I spoke a word. Vance waited for me without moving. As I came out of the alley his eyes were turned on my foot.

"I see you got it repaired," he said. "Is it well?"

"I suppose it's well," I answered coolly, for I was finished with giving him any kind of chance.

The wave of coolness reached him all right and he asked, "Did you have a faith doctor or an operation?"

I stared at him.

"Either way," he said, "it's a great pity to get fixed up just in time for the war. You should have waited a while. There's nothing to keep you out now. That is, if they're still taking Shardies."

"You're a military genius from a military school: you ought to know."

"Ah, yes, you think you've got a stranglehold on Papa because you work pretty good and got more sense than the other hands. You talked him into paying for it."

"I didn't talk him into anything."

"But the catch—do you know what the catch is? You're all fixed up to go in my place. You see? That's how you can repay Papa."

"He didn't pay for my foot."

"Is that sooooo? I suppose you took it out of your own left hind pocket."

"No, I didn't."

"Then who did? A little fairy? 'A bite to eat, A bed on hay, You may give, But nothing pay.' "

"There are still a few things you don't know."

"Really? Now he stands on two good feet."

"It didn't cost you."

"No, but my father, my poor, hard-working father."

"It didn't cost him either, because we lied about it, and the insurance company paid me when they should have been paying Victor Wells."

"So!"

I made a step toward him and he did not move. Maybe I was afraid, or maybe something else held me back. But I knew then he would never stop, that something about me unnerved him, wore him raw; I knew that someday I would kill him. We turned away from each other at the same time; he left the barn, I went home. By morning I had my mind on something else.

I was not thinking of Vance when I sat out in the early chill for the barn. Below me, in the creek bottom, a low fog lay like gray icing. I tried to make some connection between the fog and the smoke from heavy guns of the enemy, because then, for the first time, I seemed to conceive the fact that war was upon us. I remember nothing else of what happened until I reached the barn.

I saw Mr. Acroft unchain, pass through, and rechain the lot gate. He was not hurrying, and yet I knew from his walk as well as from his face that he was wild. His arms flew to and fro in a strange manner; his eyes were fixed on me; his mouth seemed ready to announce his sudden possession of the whole earth and its animals, fish and fowl.

I simply froze in my tracks and watched him approach as I might watch a train bear down upon me in a nightmare.

When he came within a few feet of me he stopped and looked me up and down. I had the distinct impression that he continued to walk and that he was speaking. But I know he was still and silent.

I was the first to speak, and because everything else seemed strange to me, I spoke strangely. "What's wrong?"

"What's wrong?" he repeated, but not in the same way. "You blab about the insurance and maybe get us both in the pen. You! When I thought I could trust you if I could trust anybody in the world. Not only your blabbing, there are other things too. I wish you'd just get out of my way and stay out. . . ." There he broke down or rather his speech broke down and I realized, as if in the wildest dream, that I held a bridle in my hand. It never occurred to me to talk back or to strike back. The bubble had burst; the rainbow was gone; and I stood there thinking I was dumb not to foresee it all.

"I'm through with you," he said.

I dropped the bridle, picked it up again and hung it on the nail where it belonged. I looked at Mr. Acroft and then I turned my back on him and all that belonged to him and walked off.

6

It was a time of utter confusion for everyone, and perhaps that is why I had no trouble getting into the army. I had supposed I would be quickly rejected, and I might have been if I had not through error got into the line of draftees rather than the line of volunteers. I must have limped enough to catch the doctor's eye and give him the idea that I was trying to get out of something. He was disagreeable and apparently bent on seeing that nothing stood between me and a khaki uniform. "You don't have to limp," he said. "I see the scar."

I merely waited for him to begin pecking on me, but I was irked by his irritableness, and disheartened by the feeling that I was not going to pass. I was ready to say whatever came to my tongue.

He grabbed my ankle roughly and said, "What caused that scar?"

"I tripped over a cow-itch vine, when I was little."

He probed a few places about my foot and looked up. "Don't you get fresh with me. Some of you clodhoppers are not half as bright as you think, not even with your shining scar. Jump up and down twenty times." Then he reeled off a long list of o-kay, o-kay, which a sergeant transferred to my medical record. Before the day was over I was in uniform. Once the matter was settled I was not so happy about it as I thought I would be.

Most of all I worried about Mama. I knew that she was sick but it had seemed to me I could do more for her away than at home. I could send her almost everything I made, which together with an allotment would be more than she had ever dreamed of.

Leaving had not been so easy. I had first of all to explain my rash and unreasonable behavior, unless I simply walked off the way Papa had done. At last I hit upon an idea, and I told Mama that Vance had accused me of stealing something. "What?" she asked immediately. I said I didn't want to talk about it but I was through with them—the Acrofts.

"No," she said, like Mr. ten Hoor, "you're not through with them. You'll never be through with them."

I could not go without seeing Mr. ten Hoor. He was there as always, a little paler perhaps, a little more broken, with the green afghan about him. The big tears ran down his face and I was shaky myself, for though we were men, we had spent a good many tender hours together in that room reading and talking and laughing and wondering about all the strange and common things of this world.

Before I left, he said, "What a terrible thing it would be if I should outlive you."

He thought I was being drafted. I had no heart for telling him the truth.

For the first few weeks I seemed not to have time to consider what had happened to me. I was so tired at night that nothing mattered, and so, actually, I was in a strange state of peacefulness. Six weeks passed and we went to a camp in South Carolina. I must have collected myself by then, and I became furious at myself for the way I had acted. Why, if I had had any guts I would have beaten Vance within an inch of his life; at least, I might have tried it. I had done the worst of all possible things; I had simply run off. Sometimes I would lie on my cot and think: Tomorrow I will take my rifle and go over the hill and hitch-hike back home and kill him, Vance, because he is not entitled to live.

And sometimes the whole matter was funny.

And I would think sometimes: I'm going to tell Esty or Wallace or Robin. Those were the ones I liked best, although two of them had never seen any cotton growing and wouldn't know what a doubletree looked like.

There was, finally, a constant gnawing inside me. I wanted to get back and redeem myself. I did not care what happened to me so long as I was given the chance to redeem myself in the eyes of Mr. Acroft. I made up many conversations between me and him, committing each word to memory. I gave myself the very best lines.

As for Vance, whatever I did to him would not be enough.

But the problem was Margo. I could not bear to make a decision about her. One day I thought I would write and the next day I hardened my heart and would not. The marching, drilling, patrolling, inspecting, and such like were nothing; it was the miserable hours of indecision that wore me down. And the long nights when I remembered this she had said or that she had said, or what I might have done, or what I should have done. It was endless . . . endless . . . and sometimes I wished we would be shipped overseas right away and I would die the common, belly-crawling death of a foot soldier.

In the spring I got part of my wish. We were shipped to England in a seven-knot convoy and on the way the ship to our starboard was sunk and the one aft of us was hit in the bow but not fatally damaged. We heard that eleven ships were lost before we reached a safe harbor. Not a safe harbor, for there was no such thing in England, but one free of U-boats anyway. I remember how the depth charges sounded like the repercussions from giant hammers. But most of all, I remember how quickly that starboard ship went down and how men fought for their lives and one hundred and six of them lost. I prayed that wherever I died it would be on the good earth, so I might return to dust and have perhaps a marker bearing my name. And people, seeing, might think: this dust was once flesh and blood, breath and thought, a miracle which no man understands. Too, I lost much of the anger which had welled in me against Vance and against Mr. Acroft. It might have been the men who died under our eyes (though I had seen nothing compared to what I would see later), or it might have been the tremendous and indescribable impact of the sea, which in its immensity reduces a matter to its proper size.

England was splendid to me in every way. And moreover, the U.S. Army was exceptionally good to me while we were bivouacked on that beautiful shepherd's hillside. Not even the swarming of the Luftwaffe disturbed my peace for long.

I became an athlete by chance, as so many things of my life had come to me by chance. One day five or six of us were sent as a loading detail to a supply depot, and we carried along a baseball to have something to do between loads. I could throw almost equally well with either hand—I was faster with my left and more accurate with my right—and it was perhaps the ambidexterousness which caught Major Calhern's eye. The Major came running out of a small gray shack that stood in the corner of the depot, and from several yards away he called, "Soldier! Soldier! You with the ball." He jerked his head, which meant I was to follow him.

I followed, into the gray shack, and wondered what punishment I would suffer for playing while on duty. In a half-hearted military manner he commanded me to strip to the waist. I was somewhat astonished, but nevertheless I obeyed, just as a slave might have stripped himself for so many lashes. I flinched when the Major rubbed his hand up and down my left arm and across my shoulders.

"You ever play ball?" he asked.

"Just in school."

"You've got what it takes. What's your name?"

I spouted off name, rank, serial number, company, the whole works. He indicated that he was finished with me and so I went out more confused than when I went in. About a week later I was transferred to a new battalion. Major Calhern sent for me and told me I was going to play baseball that summer.

I did play, and I had the time of my life. Once I pitched a double header and lost the first game, left-handed, 1–0, and lost the second game, right-handed, 10–9. Sometimes (I usually pitched left-handed) the Major would have me pitch right-handed to the right-handed hitters and the other team would squawk, but everything was for show anyway.

When the weather got cold, or rather, when it got colder, our ball playing came to an end. I went back to my original company and we spent the days leaping from landing barges onto the sandy banks of a small river. Then came the invasion of North Africa, the first and easiest of the five invasions we made. That is, it was the easiest so far as our own small sector was concerned. I don't pretend to speak for other areas where men lost their limbs and their lives.

There is not much about the war that I want to write down, because most of it seems to me now like a story I might have heard: like something Rudy might tell me if he had lived and gone through those months, years. I am sometimes amazed how I closed my eyes to what happened, how the most horrible things were horrible to me for no more than half a minute, then gone, forgotten. Too, I am amazed how I sometimes could not close my eyes and mind at all.

The most terrible thing to me was the thought of dying on a barren, gray slope in Africa, alone. And I was alone, utterly and inescapably. I might hope to live, but I could not hope to escape the aloneness. I cried when shrapnel went absolutely through one of our men. Yes, because I thought it was going to happen to me sooner or later. It was the same with Norton and Pierce and a few others: I do not remember half their names or whether it came to them in North Africa or Sicily or Salerno or Naples or Anzio or Southern France. Some whom I have forgotten I liked much better than the ones I remember. But anyway, I am sure that no one among us believed he himself would die. In war as in peace, death is for the other man.

I am sure that I got less mail than anybody in our company, perhaps less than anybody in our division. There was no one to write me except Mama and Mr. ten Hoor. During the first year away, Mr. ten Hoor wrote rather frequently but in each letter he complained of his eyesight, and finally there was a letter from him, written by his niece and postmarked in Oklahoma, saying that he was in fact blind and I must not expect to hear from him often. So at last there was only the occasional letter from Mama and sometimes I would go a month or six weeks without mail.

I will say that Mama's letters, though infrequent, were full of news, and somewhat bitter toward the Acrofts. Vance had been deferred on the grounds that he was a farmer: not a small farmer at that, for Mr. Acroft had deeded all his land to Vance. It seemed that in every letter Mama mentioned something about the Acrofts and how Vance had kept out of the army, and would usually put in a few words of how "the Lord would see they didn't git by with it."

Mr. Acroft, of course, knew the members of the draft board and he knew how to get things done. I remember when I thought about it (after one of Mama's letters) I would have a strange feeling about Mr. Acroft, and I could not help but wish I had somebody willing to do that for me, whether it was ever done or not. I never really blamed Mr. Acroft for pulling strings, but I often blamed Vance for letting him pull them. Besides, I kept the Acrofts out of my mind as much as I could.

When I heard that Margo was married I went on for weeks pretending it was not so. Finally I admitted it to myself but pretended it did not matter. I simply let everything fester inside me, and perhaps that, as much as anything, was my undoing.

It was Mr. ten Hoor who first broke the news that Margo was married. It was a long letter, the last I ever got from him in his own handwriting. Even if I did not have the letter, it seems to me I would remember it almost word for word. It began, "My dear lad, Margo has married another man."

He went on for pages telling me not to be hurt, recalling times we had spent together, and adding a paragraph here and there about somebody in The House. And here is how the letter ended: "My dear lad, this may be my last letter to you so I feel the need to speak very frankly about some church matters. I am a member of no church, but I was brought up in the church atmosphere and early was taught that man is unutterably evil; that there is not, intrinsically, one pulse beat of good in him from the time his umbilical cord is snapped until the time he draws his last breath. He may visit the sick on Wednesday, but come Saturday he will go to a dance and lose his soul; he may give generously to the poor, but then he will keep back something for wine; he may read with sympathy the trials of Job, but then he will turn next to a movie house where no good is ever to be found. To be quite frank about it, not very many people are going to get to Heaven. A sad thought, but nevertheless a true one (if you doubt this preacher, just ask some other good one). Now most of those holding tickets for the Pearly Gates are Baptists, but one has to be fair and broadminded and admit there will be a few others sprinkled about (did I say sprinkled?); and of every thousand, the ratio would be something like this: Baptists—900; Methodists—42; Presbyterians—34; Campbellites—14; Episcopalians—9; Catholics—1; Jews—.001; which allows for Christ himself, on the assumption there will be a total of one million and one. My dear lad, you can check my arithmetic. I am tired and may have made an error. *Enfin,* do not worry that Margo has flown; and above all, never let the wolves of Grace devour you."

That was the last of Mr. ten Hoor's letters. Then one day there was a letter from Aunt Pardy, a short letter, like forgotten flack out of a rainsoaked sky. She wrote that Mama had died of tuberculosis. It seems now that I felt nothing for days, that my whole body was like a cold stone. One thing pulls. Another thing pulls. But at last comes the limit of endurance, and you break like glass, for there is nothing to hold the measly little splinters together any more.

That summer Rome fell.

I remember the city as I remember no other: colonnaded courts, museums, galleries, amphitheaters, paintings, mosaics, monuments, catacombs, chapels, and beautiful shops. We had one happy spell of it and then we were pulled back to prepare for Southern France.

I am ashamed to say I had not thought much about Mama's funeral. I mean, I had not thought about who arranged the many details and who paid for it. I knew, from Aunt Pardy, the time and the place (next to Rudy) and that was about all I knew. I never once thought of writing McFarland Funeral Home, Cross City, and asking who had paid, nor of asking anything. I do not understand myself on that matter, so I cannot expect others to understand. It is odd to me, even yet, and therefore must be totally unreasonable to others. I might explain it by saying we had gone through some hard fighting, had lost many men, and every day, or hour, each man expected the worst for himself. Still, such is not enough explanation to myself and could hardly be enough for others.

One day, before Southern France, I had a letter from Vance Acroft, R.F.D. # 1, Cross City. I knew immediately it had something to do with the funeral, but I was puzzled that the letter should come from Vance instead of Mr. Acroft. I remembered, however, one of Mama's letters in which she gave me a long account of how Mr. Acroft had gone to Missouri, to one of the Springs-health-centers; of how people were saying he had cancer, though to her notion it was mostly a stunt to get everything into Vance's hands and keep him out of the army.

I opened the letter, which contained a small ledger sheet with the letterhead, McFARLAND FUNERAL HOME, and a smaller page on which Vance had written:

July 15, 1944
Since I have heard nothing from you I am enclosing Mc-Farland's bill which I paid, $321.00. If you haven't the money please be kind enough to acknowledge full amount and pay as soon as possible.

Vance Acroft

I cannot say there was anything wrong with his letter, though I know full well he intentionally left off "Dear Max" and "Sincerely."

I had about eighty dollars. My first decision was to borrow the money and repay it a little each month. But that meant explaining a great many things which I had no heart to

explain. I sent seventy-one dollars to Vance on the first day
of August, with the note: "Enclosed is seventy-one dollars,
partial payment of my debt. I acknowledge a balance of
$250.00."

On the first of every month thereafter, for five months, I
sent fifty dollars to Vance. Simply a money order and nothing else, until the final payment, to which I added this note:

Dear Vance,

I believe this is the final payment of the $321.00. I ap-
preciate your paying McFarland for me.

Sincerely,
Max

I wrote the letter because I was going to wash my hands
of the Acrofts forever. I was absolutely sincere. I did appreciate his paying McFarland, though I did not like him any
better than before. I thought it was my duty to thank him
for having taken on something which was not his responsi-
bility. There was no need to let the past make a fool of me.
Nevertheless, I got nowhere with my gesture of peace.

Back came a letter from Vance: "Your account will not be
settled until and unless you forward to me interest at 6% on
$321.00 for eight months. At that I am not charging you full
time."

I sent him a money order for twelve dollars and eighty-
four cents. And that was another thing I never got out of my
heart. I could tell no one about these matters which grew
and festered in me and destroyed any willingness ever to for-

give him. Together we were beyond redemption. Evil day
that I ever saw his face or heard his name. And yet I know,
deep in my heart, it was I who drove him to such indecencies;
I who hounded him up and down the corridors of his mind;
I who would not let him rest in peace. How strange indeed,
though all the minds in the world cannot change it. No word
can be recalled, no thought can be recast; no breath can be
redrawn. And so we move on, creeping to the earth again,
wishing tomorrow that yesterday had been a time of love.

7

IT WAS my time at last, and it came early in the
morning, much in the same way as Mr. Acroft's decree of
banishment. We were in the hills above a small village, the
name of which I do not remember if I ever knew. We had
been out since three o'clock and had spotted nothing. We
were waiting, according to orders, rehashing the old rumors
of the end and rumors of names up for rotation. The other
five in our patrol agreed that it couldn't last much longer for
me, because I had been through it all from the first landing
in North Africa: a record shared by only nine in our company.

I was lying flat on my back feeling superior and immortal,
I suppose, when an Me 109 sneaked up on us as easily as a

mosquito would come through an open window. Blue fire was spouting toward us from a sky which had been perfectly calm only three seconds before. I rolled over on my face, but even as I rolled I felt the sharp jabs in my thigh, my hip, and my side. Then I felt my tongue in the dirt. When I try to remember the hours that followed, I can recall only a hillside of snow, broken by scattered trees; and a voice saying, "Eight," over and over again.

I was picked up by a command car and carried back to the nearest hospital. A week later I was in Nice, in a room overlooking the sea, and the war seemed unbelievable to me.

In that short time I had already begun to forget faces, to wonder if such and such occurrence had been real or my imagination, and this—above all—if the war had been worth the price.

My wounds healed quickly, leaving ugly scars but apparently no permanent ill effects. In April I was not only well enough to walk along the beach but I also took rather long hikes into the countryside, which is incredibly beautiful. Sometimes I would go alone and sometimes I would go with any of the army personnel who felt inclined to walk.

It was by chance again that my life found direction for what I was to do after the war. There was already much postwar talk and much speculation as to jobs and education and homes and what not. I had no plans, though there was inside me the old gnawing urge to get back home, and home meant the Acroft place and the three-room, tin-top house, which, though I did not know it, lay in ashes at the time. Still, I was not anxious to leave Nice and a life which was altogether comfortable, and in many respects actually affluent.

One day a group of us managed to get possession of a command car and went to Monte Carlo to see, and gamble in, the famous Casino. I am not much of a gambler and so spent most of the evening watching and listening. It was perhaps the most fascinating time of my life. Never have I witnessed such various expressions of hope and joy and misery and disappointment. Not that alone, but also the anxiousness even for a stranger, the roulette wheel coming slowly to rest, the pitiful little exclamations of ruin, the long reach of the croupier in his black apparel, and the noncommittal expressions, "Faîtes vos jeux" and "Rien ne va plus." I went from table to table, drinking in some new aspects of humanity, until a hand tapped my shoulder.

I turned and was face to face with someone vaguely familiar, and I might have recognized him immediately if his colonel's insignia had not frightened me. I was not accustomed to having colonels tap me on the shoulder.

He announced rather calmly, "I thought you were dead, Harper."

I recognized him as the Major Calhern who had made a baseball pitcher out of me during an English tour. He called over a captain and a lieutenant and horse and explained that I was at the moment a mere corporal, but give me three

years and I'd be the mainstay on the mound for the New
York Giants; that he had been a Giant scout for six years and
he'd never seen a lefty, my age, with as much control; that
maybe the nurse didn't know it but the captain certainly
understood how any southpaw with control would be as hard
to keep out of the majors as it would be to keep Jesse Owens
on the other side of a ten-foot ditch if the boy really and
truly wanted to leap across it; that he had already written
Hershel Winters about me, twice in fact, and the first thing
I was to do when I got to the States was to go see Hershel.
He gave me a great deal of advice, told me how to reach
Hershel, whom he was going to write again, and warned me
I'd better take care of my arm, but to get in shape for Hershel
should he want to take a look, and not to worry about my
future.

Colonel Calhern was quite drunk.

I convinced myself he had not uttered a sober syllable, and
decided there was perhaps no such person as Hershel
Winters. Nevertheless, I was pepped up, and was so anxious
to believe the impossible that I spent more than twenty dollars for one baseball and a wornout mitt. I paid little French
boys one hundred francs an hour to catch me or try to. The
first week was not so bad, but when I began to throw harder,
tragedy set in: two dislocated fingers, and one broken thumb.
I had to stop it, though they would never have stopped. They
were hungry, and a dislocated finger was probably more de-
sirable than an empty belly. I can still hear their voices

begging for another chance, "Joe! Joe! Regarde! Regarde, Joe!" I paid all of them again and told them not to come back, but they came back. "Joe! Joe!" Jean-Claude was the best and the bravest and it was two days before I knew his thumb was broken. I took him to an army doctor.

I lost several days of practice before I found a sergeant, with a cast on his ankle, who liked baseball well enough to catch me.

Every week I expected to sail for the States. If I had not had a baseball and a wild notion in my head, I might have become bored and miserable.

So at last the European war was over! There was much rejoicing among the French, and many warm-hearted offers of food and wine and friendship and understanding. The Americans seemed rather calm about it all and rather distant, or else they were perfect vandals. To me, there was something quite sad about the ending of the war.

I have learned that the things I expect most are often unreasonably delayed, and the things I expect least are often the most certain to arrive. So it happened that I waited and waited for orders home, and when they finally came I went by train to Le Havre, with a short stay in Paris. A few days of beautiful weather at sea and then we were coming into New York harbor. Oh, warriors and heroes! We got quite a welcome.

The sea had sobered me considerably, and I had decided the idea of my ever being a ball player was ridiculous. The army team on which I had starred could probably be matched on a hundred, maybe a thousand, sandlots in New York.

I knew I would have four days in New York before going on to the separation center. It was a miserable time, because I could not make up my mind what to do. I was not a ball player, and it did not seem reasonable to me that someone would gamble money on what I might become. I could not bring myself to call Hershel Winters, though I walked streets for hours carrying in my hand a card with the address and telephone number of his office. Each day, however, I went nearer and nearer his office. Then one morning I went to his office door. I read his name; I read the office number: 412. I turned away. I went back four or five or maybe six times before I managed to push the door open and enter.

Name please?

That much was done.

Was Mr. Winters expecting you?

I didn't know, but he had a letter about me.

You're a ball player?

Yes.

A letter about you? A letter from whom?

From Colonel Richard Calhern . . .

Oh, but how some names shatter the walls of Jericho!

Mr. Winters would see me at two o'clock.

I noticed then that she was really very pretty. She smiled as I went out.

She smiled again, when I came back exactly three hours later.

Mr. Winters looked like a druggist. He looked like a high-school chemistry teacher. He looked like a shoe salesman. He looked like a train conductor. He looked like anything and everything except a man who hired ball players. He was too small for his chair.

"What do you want, Harper?"

"I want to be a ball player," I said.

He cried out an oath and threw his little body backward and laughed and laughed, and wanted to know if Colonel Calhern had told me what to say, because, he added, "When I ask them that, they usually tell me how many thousands."

We got along well. He wanted to know when I would be out of the army and if I could go to Minnie Hill, Alabama, for the last three weeks of the season. I said yes to everything he proposed.

I was to receive four thousand dollars for signing a contract! Almost half a mile of dollar bills! All without pitching one single ball.

I was drunk. I cannot describe what I felt when I left that office. I caught a bus and rode and rode. I was rich. I wanted to pay the bus fare of every man, woman, and child. I wanted to tell them about my good fortune. I changed buses again and again. I rode the subway for the first time in my life. I got lost. I thought of Margo. I imagined that she was with me. I was unbelievably happy and totally insane.

I saw a man who looked like Papa. I spoke to him and he turned quickly away.

I bought a pound of cashew nuts, all I had ever wanted.

I went to the telephone and tried to put through a call to Margo. The operator said there was no such number listed. I said, "No, I'm sure she hasn't got a phone."

I was homesick. I thought of a tree below the big springs on the Acroft place where I had carved my initials by standing forty feet away and throwing rocks. And Rudy had given me a quarter (which I had given to him out of Mr. ten Hoor's money) to carve a big R for him.

I walked up and down Broadway, hypnotized by the big lights and crowds and the good fortune I carried in my heart. I searched face after face, young and old, beautiful and ugly, and in all that scrambled, hurried, uncommitted throng there was not one to whom I could tell my secret. Where were they going that they had no time to listen? And where were the people of my life anyway? It would have been the same if I had walked the streets of Cross City.

Hear ye, hear ye! Lift your eyes toward Times Square and read: MAX HARPER, brilliant young southpaw, signed today by New York Giants. Oh, you lucky Giants! As he signed his contract, young Harper (veteran of North Africa, Sicily, Salerno, Anzio, Southern France) said, "I am indeed grateful to Mr. Winters and to Major . . . uh . . . Colonel Richard Calhern . . . for this opportunity . . ."

Go on, you blind, insensitive people. There is too much

light around you. You would never notice if all the stars in heaven faded out.

I said those words in my mind, but my heart was with the million-footed city, the scorching sidewalks, the sea of faces, the big lights, and the whirlwind of life that went past me again and again. One day they would come to know my name, and flock to see me; they would love me and in turn my heart would embrace them all. O bright, inextinguishable dream.

My feet burned, my body ached, and yet I walked on and on. The only ones with whom I might share my secret were the Acrofts. I even wished for Vance, and felt in my heart a wave of kindness toward him.

At midnight I left the city which I know I am never to see again.

A week later I was out of the army and instead of going to Cross City, I went directly to Minnie Hill. It was a Class C League, depleted because of the war, and stocked with seventeen-year-olds or veterans much too slow to follow a fast ball. On the tenth day there I pitched four innings, allowed four singles and one unearned run. I relieved only three other times until the end of the season and allowed only one run to cross the plate, that on a wild pitch.

On the last day of the season, which was Labor Day, I relieved in the ninth inning with one man out and a man on first and third. I struck out the first two batters with eight pitches, and the Congressional Medal of Honor couldn't have meant more to me. A 3-2 ball game which we won and the kids came pulling at me. It is a memory I must hold onto until the very last. The manager said I ought to make Nashville next year, and the great big Italian catcher smothered me in his arms as if I had been the least of his nine kids. There must be such a thing as glory, and I must have had a spoonful of it that day, which was enough to set wild notions in my head again and bring to the foreground that bright, inextinguishable dream. Only the day before I had got my check for four thousand dollars.

On the way home that night, on the bus, it was hard to fight back the tears. Life was so wonderful that I buried all ill will toward the Acrofts. Was there anyone in the world whom I did not love? Next year I would be pitching for Nashville! That's Double A ball, sonny.

Soon I would be able to *see* Margo.

Part Four

I

MR. TEN HOOR used to say we are mere puppets and wherever our minds or our hands or our feet touch, there we leave a string to tug after us. Anyway, I was drawn back to Cross City and the Acroft place by something stronger than rope or chain.

I got to Cross City in mid-morning. I caught a ride as far as the Poor Farm, which I walked by but did not enter, for Mr. ten Hoor was no longer there. I was not satisfied until I had placed my feet on Acroft ground.

I cannot remember whether I knew then our old house had burned, or whether I simply came upon its ashes and the twisted old stove and the andirons and the buckles and nails and bed springs and the various grotesque remains. I do not remember being surprised, and still I do not know how I could have known.

I walked around and around the rock chimney and probed in the ashes, which were dry and dusty. I could see people picking cotton in the small creek bottom below, but they were too far away and too busy to notice. I turned my back to them, sat down on a rock which had been a pillar, and my tears dug small holes in the ashes. It was a bright, winy day, and I sat for a long time while the sweat popped out around my neck and on my forehead. I brought them back and they walked before me in the clear sunlight. I saw their faces and I heard their voices, while my whole being wallowed in the ashes of despair.

I reached a new low, but I arose and went away strengthened. I must have sensed that something tremendous and pleasant was about to happen to me before my final undoing. In my numbered days ahead I was to come to know that nothing on earth is so beautiful as a beautiful family. I came upon them by accident: these five people who loved and were loved; who gave generously in their own circle as well as to others; who went about their daily tasks calmly, without fuss and with humor. They lived not by rigid rules, but by a well-defined order, the center of which was Victor Wells.

Because I had seen Victor mostly at the sawmill I thought of him as a timber man, not a farmer. I was a little bit surprised to find him in the cotton field which we had once worked. But there he was standing between two white rows, his hands full of bolls, a broad grin on his face, waiting for me. We never shook hands, because that would have suggested we were strangers; but he stood there looking me up and down, and I felt then, for the first time, I was home from the war. A few words passed between us and he looked across his field at cotton finer than anything we had ever grown there. He moved a few steps and I noticed the old limp from his injured knee. A sharp pain went through me and sweat broke out on my forehead. Something inside me said: You thought the war had erased all that, but it didn't. He must have noticed the sudden sweat. He shook his head. "Hot, ain't it?"

I nodded. And as if to keep him away from my thoughts, I said, "This is the finest crop I've ever seen here."

He was immensely pleased at what he knew was the truth. "You might not think it," he said, "but we're picking eighty pounds to the row. It don't take long to get a bale."

He was several yards ahead of the others, as if that were the place he expected a father to be. Next was his twelve-year-old son, Claude, and a yard or two farther back, his wife and daughter, Anne, who was almost sixteen. Six-year-old Carroll was a hundred yards away with a flour sack on one shoulder and an air rifle on the other. He came up to look at me, his great blue eyes shining, and then he retreated and sat down on the row behind his mother.

"You don't know my family, do you?" Victor said.

They stopped long enough to hear their names and then went back to work, all but Carroll, who rolled over and laughed at the sound of his name.

Victor waited for me to appraise them. Again, I saw his dark, steady eyes reflect a whole world of peacefulness. It seemed to me then I had no reason to be afraid of the past and what we had done—Mr. Acroft and I—for there was no reason to believe Victor would ever know. I was filled with sudden security and the wish, maybe even the need, to be near Victor. After all, had I really done him any wrong? In any case, I meant to make up for it somehow.

I dropped to my knees and began to pick on his row, as if that would be the beginning of my repayment. When Victor began picking, I noticed again the stiffness in his knee. I thought: it is best to overlook it, never to mention his knee. But the next minute I was asking, "Does it bother you much? Your knee?"

"Naw. Not much. Only sometimes I can tell when it's going to rain. Hurts more in wet weather." He laughed. It was such careless, genuine laughter I thought again there was no reason for me to worry.

I stayed with them that night. Maybe he knew I had nowhere else to go, and maybe that was why the next morning he told me he could always raise more than he could gather and he'd be glad if I stayed. I did stay, and made my home in a neat little side room which his wife furnished for me.

Victor got up every morning at four o'clock. I would hear his steps in the hall and then hear him make his way across the large kitchen to the stove. In two or three minutes, never more than four, he would have the fire kindled. Then, if it was cold, I would soon hear a roaring in the fireplace. For the next few minutes all would be perfectly quiet. Out of the silence would come, "Lillie, Lillie . . . best fire in the kitchen you ever seen."

When I heard it that first morning I thought it was par-

tially performed for me (because I know people are sometimes kinder to intimates when a stranger is present). But I
was to hear it every morning of the world, the same genuine,
good-humored tone; and I was not long in learning the truth.

She would answer a word or two, so quietly I never heard,
and a few minutes later she would be moving briskly about
the kitchen. Then I would know I could get up.

Victor would be washing and he would sort of shake his
head at me. We always went together to the barn to feed. He
never said good morning to me and I never said good morning to him. We never said anything to each other until the
crib was unlocked and the first ear of corn fell into the
basket, after which we said whatever came to our minds.

We worked hard, right through until sundown on Satur-
days and I never knew I could pick so much cotton. My back
ached and my fingers reached for bolls in my dreams. After
the cotton came corn, potatoes, peanuts; and after that, a
few days of fall plowing. Then bad weather set in. We were
finished until after Christmas, when he was to start logging.
In the meantime, we meant to spend a few days hunting.
We had made a good start when the fateful day came: the
fourteenth of December.

But I have not put down all that happened during that
fall. And if you do not understand that time and Victor and
his family and my feeling toward them, then you may not
understand what happened on December the fourteenth.

For my part, I do not understand why one man commands

respect above all others: a man who is not a leader, who is
not clever, who is in no way a hero. Maybe it was the simple
fact that he was completely satisfied. But there he was, and
sometimes I would think: there he will always be. When he
was sawing down a tree he was like a god; when he was
telling an ugly joke he was the same; and when his children
climbed on him for his affection he was the same. Too, he
had left his mark on those around him.

I thought of his wife, whom I called Miss Lillie, as all
woman and mother. She was plump and quick, systematic
and thorough, but never hurried. She was lovable to me
because she was equally affectionate toward daughter and
sons. From the beginning she treated me as her own child,
which was reason enough to love her. I remember the first
Sunday when I came to stay with them. I had told no one,
but early in the morning I got ready to go see Rudy's and
Mama's grave. As I stepped off the porch she handed me two
bouquets of flowers. How could she have known? Except, of
course, it was that infinite kindness which belongs only to a
woman. When, by chance, I used to hear from her little ugly
words, which one usually expects only from men, I would
be pleased. It kept from her the false aura of perfection. For
the same reason, I liked to hear Victor curse now and then.

Claude was a little devil and still he was like Victor. When
he used to come running out the doorway headed for school,
his short, golden hair slicked down, his blue eyes burning,
his tongue playing across a fever blister or two, I would

think of Rudy. He used to ask me much about the war. I have sometimes seen him get very nervous about the things I would tell, as if I must one day go through all of it again. It was a great satisfaction to believe he loved me.

Carroll was everyone's darling, and spoiled, but lovable and polite. Still, he was Victor's boy really, and I was only his toy hero, which, however, was no small satisfaction.

In Anne one could see the miracle from day to day. She was beginning to be beautiful. In three short months I saw the immense change, which would not be finished for two or three years. But already she was a young woman, full of fire and kindness, to which could be added unusual intelligence. She knew exactly what she could get and what she could not get from Daddy, whom she would worship if he would allow it. I thought it strange that she and her mother should be such chums and should get along so well together. But then, the whole family was an oddity to me: five people who seemed never to quarrel or bicker! Victor told me he had quarreled with his wife only once in the eighteen years they had been married. No. Not a real quarrel. She wanted to do something, to go somewhere. He simply forbade it with the warning that if she went she might as well take her clothes. She didn't go. I remember how he grinned when he told me about it.

Anne has his grin, and though she is quite feminine it makes her a bit tomboyish. In the beginning she had very little to say to me, while the boys, Carroll anyway, had fully accepted me from the third day. Claude took up with me well enough but he never hesitated to let me know that I was in most cases a notch below his father. When he came from school one day and heard that I had picked twelve more pounds of cotton than Victor, he simply refused to believe it. He got a Yes from his question, "He didn't do it, did he, Daddy?" Nevertheless, his faith remained firm and he insisted there must have been some trick. But the next day, when he came home with the same question, I was forty pounds behind and suddenly wise to the back-breaking pace Victor had set all day; and a little outdone at the way both of them laughed at me.

It was the middle of October when the ice first broke between me and Anne. She had been given fifty algebra problems for the week, forty-nine of which she had worked; but with one she could make no headway and the failure was driving her into a fit of ill temper. I saw her anxiety and left the Chinese checkerboard with the others and offered to help her. To her surprise I worked the problem in a few seconds. She cried out my name in a very pleasant way and the whole family stopped, as if to give me a new appraisal. She ran to Victor and hugged and kissed him; which caused Claude to say, "Silliest thing I ever saw. You ought to hug Max."

Without hesitation she carried out his advice and I sat there with my cheeks burning, my tongue paralyzed, and perspiration leaping out all over me. She was not a child to me, and each passing day made it more difficult for me to separate the real Anne, the child, from the image of the future Anne. Besides, she was almost sixteen.

Lots of nights I would go out walking alone, usually in the vast acres of cut-over woods, where Mr. Acroft and I used to ride on horseback. Sometimes I would stop at an old Indian mound and from there I could see the Acroft house, and Margo's house down the road, and Victor's house.

One night I was sitting on the mound when Anne walked up to me. She was there standing before me, with her black hair thrown back, and her black eyes appraising me, before I noticed. I jumped up. I was afraid. The truth was: I was afraid of Victor.

"What are you doing up here?" I said, quickly, nervously.

"It's not your mound," she answered.

"You can't stay here!"

"I reckon I can," she said, and sat down. "I'll stay here as long as I want to."

I sank down heavily. "You don't understand," I said. "I mean . . ."

"I do understand. You came up to look at Margo's house. And you've been up here before. I know."

I did not bother to deny anything. I was uneasy and wondering what would happen when we went back together. There was a minute of silence, so long that it seemed I could have walked all the way back to the house.

"Did you know I could sing?" she asked.

"No."

"Do you want to hear me?"

"No."

"Not even one of my own songs?"

"No."

"Of course, it's silly and you'll laugh, but I'm going to sing it anyway. But I've got to explain it to you. I made it up during the war when so many planes kept coming over." She moved to her knees and sang:

> My love is like a silver bird,
> A splendid aeroplane;
> He went beyond the wind and clouds
> And way beyond the rain.
>
> Come back to me my aeroplane,
> Come back my silver bird;
> Come back to me and take my hand
> And never say a word.
>
> Oh, stop, my heart! Don't make a sound;
> Listen for the drone.
> I know that he will come again;
> He'll never leave me alone.

"Now?" she asked.

"Now what?" I said, but I was weak and trembly. Whether her singing was good or bad it had torn at me, shaken me, and I wondered what on earth I would do if Victor came upon us. I was cold. I could hardly talk. "What would Victor say if he knew you were up here?"

"Oh, he wouldn't say much. I don't care if he knows. I'll tell him."

"You don't do any such thing!" I said.

"I will. Who can stop me?"

"But . . ."

"But nothing. I'll tell him I came and I'll tell him I'm coming back again . . . if I want to."

"You're foolish!"

"I'm not foolish." She got up. "It's all right. Daddy likes you too."

She left me there, and after the sound of her steps died away it was the quietest place I had ever known. A little while later I was startled to realize I was crying. Maybe I was just a child, or maybe it was just too much to live with Victor's family. I can't help it about his knee, I said; he's got everything, everything in the world I would like to have.

2

I HAD lived at Victor's for a week before I came face to face with an Acroft. I had not exactly avoided them, but I had made no effort to see them either. Mr. Acroft was in Missouri suffering a serious stomach ailment which everyone believed to be cancer. Mrs. Acroft divided her time between home and Missouri, but her whereabouts were usually unknown, for even when she was at home she stayed in the house all day and was rarely seen. Vance was wherever you found him, at the barn, in Cross City, Chicago, Texarkana. If you needed tin for a new roof, he could get it for you; if you wanted a new automobile, he could get it for you; if you wanted an extra hundred pounds of sugar for canning, he could get it for you. All at a price.

Margo lived in a new house about a quarter of a mile from the Acroft place, and about a mile from Victor's house. She had two daughters, one a little over two years old and one a little less than a year. Her husband, who had got into the war late, was still in the Pacific on a landing craft. He was a lieutenant (junior grade) according to Margo's own words but many people spoke of him as MacArthur's counterpart. From Victor's house (which was known as the Murchison old place) we could see Margo's house, one corner of it, and at night we could see the porch light which she always burned.

One afternoon, when it had rained and we could not work, I went walking along the sawmill road which I had traveled so often with Mr. Acroft. When I left the mill place, which was too quiet for me, I returned along the mill road, and so came upon Margo's house.

She was in the yard clipping or thinning a streak of verbena when we saw each other—she saw me almost the moment I saw her. She lifted a pair of scissors and shaded her eyes, and I have a feeling she was halfway expecting me.

When I came closer she called out, "I'm a good mind to hug your neck, Max Harper."

I came along the walk and said I wouldn't mind.

Nevertheless, we remained two or three yards apart, and she began to talk quickly about having heard that I was back; and why hadn't I been to see some of them before now? Did I know she had two daughters, exactly like Bob? I must sit down (on the porch) and she would bring some ice tea, and in a little while the girls would be awake. I had the impression of a meeting between cousins who had been fond of each other in their childhood. I was peeved and so would say very little.

"You haven't seen Vance?" she asked.

"No."

"You must be avoiding him."

"I'm not avoiding him. I guess we don't have much to say to each other."

"You're too hard on Vance."

"In what way?"

"In the same way Papa was. He always treated me like a boy and Vance like a girl. But he couldn't stand it if Vance acted the least bit weak about anything. I reckon he wanted him to be the best millhand without working and the best soldier without ever going to war. Oh, I don't know. But it seems to me Vance has his side of the story somehow . . . somewhere. . . . Maybe they were always partial to me. Papa, anyway. And I've seen him let you do things he wouldn't let Vance do. Oh, I tell you I don't know!" She seemed at the end of a long, long road. "Come and see my daughters. They're waking up now."

They were not waking up. She was simply anxious and ill at ease.

But I saw them (How long ago that day seems!), asleep on the same bed. And I saw the picture of Bob, and I was so uncomfortable I left as quickly as I could. I made it a point to remember she had asked nothing of what had happened to me in the years which stood so certainly between us.

While we were feeding that night, Victor asked me where I had been, and I said I had gone down by the mill place and had come back by Margo's. He said, in a sort of devilish way, "Did you have a nice visit?" I was mad at Margo, or something, so I took my spite out on him. But I was all right by suppertime.

A few days later Vance came to the field where we were picking cotton. He spoke to me first, as agreeably as anybody could, and I answered as I would have answered anybody. I can't remember feeling anything toward him. He seemed to me to be unusually nervous and fidgety. He smoked two or three cigarettes, or rather, something like a third of each one and then threw it away only to bring out another in a few seconds. He asked what classification Victor had got on three previous bales of cotton, and a few more questions of that nature. He asked me which I liked best, soldiering or cotton picking. I said that might depend on where I was soldiering.

He said, "You did get into some of it, didn't you?"

I said, "Yes, some."

He said, "Yes, but you're going to find out we made a grave mistake."

"How?" I asked.

"The Germans had a point. Take Communism, for example."

"You take it," I said.

"Listen, I know what I'm talking about. I know what's happening in this country. One of these days we'll be in the same boat—not the same boat, but one like it."

"What do you mean?"

"Haven't you heard of the race question? White versus black, you know?" He turned to Victor. "Don't let him fool you, Victor. I don't care where he's been. Hitler had a point." With that, he threw his cigarette away and went off.

I was not mad. I was just sick at my stomach, literally. I have never before or since had so much of the war come back to me all at once: blood and thunder and smoke and blue flesh and snow and bones. I half knelt, half lay in the cotton middle. When Victor noticed me he asked what was the matter. "I don't know. I just turned sick."

He came back a few steps. Sweat was dripping off my neck. He took a handful of cotton and dried my neck and face and tried to make me go to the house, but I knew it would pass in a matter of minutes. And it did. Victor never made any comment on the things Vance had said.

Maybe a week or two went by before Vance came to the field a second time and called Victor off for a private talk. They must have talked for thirty minutes and every time I looked that way Vance was either kicking his heel into the ground or pacing up and down the cotton middle. I had the feeling he might disintegrate any minute. After Vance was gone I wondered whether Victor would tell me what passed between them. I knew almost nothing about Victor's business. He had been a tenant on his father's place at the time he worked at the mill; a year after I went into the army he had bought the Murchison old place, forty acres, and had rented the Big Springs place from Vance, which was the forty we had worked. That was all I knew about Victor's business.

Vance had been gone an hour or more when Victor sat down on his sack and waited for me to catch up. "That boy is in trouble," he said. I asked what kind of trouble, or some such question.

"I don't know," Victor said. "But something's wrong. He said he had to raise some money. He wanted to sell me this forty acres."

"Must be something wrong," I said. "I never heard of an Acroft selling land."

"He's asking twenty-five hundred dollars. Two thousand will buy it, and it's worth three. I'll show you why." He pointed to the four big springs which flowed the year around and fed a small bottom which had not been worked since we moved there. "There's fifteen or twenty acres of the best pasture land a man could ever hope for. It takes water, moisture, to make a good pasture."

"Why don't you buy it?" I asked.

"I can't. I'm just not in shape to. He wants cash. That's big money to me."

"If you want it," I said, "I know where you can get the money."

"Where?"

"From me."

He thought I was joking him, because he didn't know any more about my business than I knew about his. "You buy it," he said.

"I might," I answered. "If you don't."

I think he didn't know whether to believe me or not and so he went back to work. I could think of nothing else the rest of the day, and for the two days that followed. I was obsessed with the idea of owning land which had been in Acroft hands. One might think I wanted it because we had lived there and worked the place and it was home to me. Maybe that mattered, but that was not the heart of the matter. Was it not a great triumph for me to take land out of the hands of Vance Acroft?

And still another consideration: I saw in the land a chance to tie myself to Victor and his family. When I went off to play ball in the spring, I would go with the idea of coming back. My plans were rather specific: one fall I would come back and Anne would be a young woman, not a child. It seems a bit wild to me now, but at that time all these things seemed quite reasonable.

One night I explained to Victor how much money I had and where it came from. Again I offered him money for the land, but hoped desperately he would not take it. I added that if he didn't want it, I was going to buy it, and of course he could work it as long as he liked, and in any way he liked.

Before the matter was settled, I know he sensed how much I wanted the land. "You ought to have it," he kept saying. "You want it and you ought to have it. You've lived there. It's no reason why you ought to put up money to buy me something you want. And I know you want it."

And I got it, for two thousand dollars, exactly as Victor had said. He went with me to the Chancery Clerk's office to witness the signing of the deed. At first, Vance was agreeable enough toward me but was irritable toward the secretary, who seemed slow in typing the abstract. When it was over and the deed was in my pocket, he took my check and said, "You're stealing that land, you know. It's worth twice that much. I'll prove it by Victor. Victor, is he stealing it?"

"That's between you two," Victor said.

"Yeah, you're stealing it," Vance said. Then he put the last ugly period to the transaction by waving my check and saying, "This better not bounce, Harper."

Maybe Mr. Acroft knew at the time about the sale and

maybe he didn't, or maybe one does not worry about such things when death is gnawing the vitals. In any case, the land was in Vance's name and he was able to give a clear deed. There was probably still some fear that Vance might be drafted into the army, as he was unmarried and without dependents, unless he claimed dependency for his father and mother. The chief question in my mind was, why would Vance have to have money? Surely he had made something during the war, for I had already heard several references to his black-market business. Besides, he should have made something from the farm (I understood the sawmill was sold soon after I left). But I had to agree with Victor: Vance had acted as if he were in desperate circumstances.

Later, we heard he had lost lots of money in a black-market sugar deal in Texarkana, and the amount was usually quoted as four thousand and four hundred dollars, though it sometimes reached a high of eight thousand. According to the story, Vance himself helped load the sugar onto a trailer truck, counted the sacks, handed over the cash, only to find out a few hundred miles later that his truck was loaded with so many tons of white sand. And that was how Vance ran out of cash and how I came to own land which had been in Acroft hands for more than a century.

From the beginning I had an uneasy feeling about the whole matter. First of all, Victor was the logical one to own it. And next, I wondered what Mr. Acroft would think; yes, I even worried about it, though I still remembered his decree of banishment. But I also remembered he had lied for me, and in a way was that not more than telling the truth for me? It was he who had made me whole in body; he who had laid down part of himself; he who had created for me the unextinguishable dream of fame and honor—not Major Calhern; and yet again, it was to some degree his money with which I had bought his land. He had given and given and I had taken and taken from him. If he had driven me into outer darkness, had he not also driven me beyond it into a new light? When I tried to talk to Victor about these things, he took my side, which helped, and he said, "Somebody was going to buy it. You didn't push anybody into anything." But the ugly little demons danced in my head and made me uneasy when I was alone, in the darkness, and let my mind dwell on the matter.

When I worked beside Victor I was all right. When I walked among the springs that belonged to me, I was all right. I said, this earth is mine! mine! The Acrofts have earth for their feet, plenty of it, hundreds of acres, and I have—after all—only forty measly acres, but it is mine! mine! And I will hold on to it forever. It will be mine when my name is familiar to every schoolboy who has ever tried to throw a curve. I will be famous. I will be the beginning of something new for those of our name who never owned a foot of land. I have been chosen for this. I have been given the coat of many colors, but I will avoid the pit. There will be no pit for me.

I went often to the mound. Sometimes I found Anne there ahead of me. But I was no longer afraid. And I no longer cared about the lights in the Acroft house or Margo's house; only Victor's house mattered.

Anne sensed everything. She knew all the crooked little pieces of the puzzle had at last fallen into order. She knew well enough. I was so happy that my heart seemed to run wild even in my sleep. Only now and then in that bright, incredible time a small shadow would appear: I would be working beside Victor and I would see him limp and I would wonder if he would ever know. But it was a small worry, fleeting as a moth, a passing breath of doubt. Of course, he would never know; and the magic appeared again.

So autumn went. Who can say I did not reap enough happiness in that short season to last a man forever? Then winter came in its appointed time.

3

AT LAST Vance came to me to ask for something. It was the second week of last December (ninety-nine years ago it seems), a raw, whirling day too cold for rain. I was coming back from Mr. Harmon's place where I had been to buy two beagle hounds for rabbit hunting. I had cut through the woods, partially to give the dogs a chance to track and par-

tially to avoid Margo's house. I was surprised when I saw
Vance standing on a knoll ahead of me. I remember exactly
what was in my mind: I was thinking that somewhere, sometime in my childhood I had been told it was a sin to buy a
dog, that there was something in the Bible to that effect;
and I was thinking that I must remember to ask Victor if he
had ever heard of such a thing; and I was thinking that
Victor would have a good answer, because he always had a
good answer for such questions.

Vance lost no time in getting down to his business. He
said he had been to Victor's looking for me, had been looking for me for a week, and why was I avoiding him?

"I didn't know you'd been looking for me," I said. "What
do you want?"

"I want that land back."

"What do you want it back for?"

"Don't you know an Acroft don't sell land?" I must admit
he did not, at the time, sound offensive.

I said, "What did you sell it for then?"

"I had to. I had a bad piece of luck."

"You must've had a good piece of luck if you can buy it
back."

"Not exactly. It's been our land a long time. Papa wants
it back."

"What did he say about it?"

"He wants it back, Max. He's not going to live long."

"I've heard. I'm sorry about that."

"I believe you'll see my side of it."

"I do."

"I tell you the truth: I'm not asking you to do this for me. It's for Papa."

"I'll tell you the truth: I'd do it for him a lot quicker than I'd do it for you."

"I know you don't like me," he said. "I don't blame you. I've wondered lots of times why we couldn't get along."

"Have you?"

"Yes, I have. You see one way and I see another. You're a little bit too honest, Max, which is all right if you can hold out at it. But you can't. And I can't. A man like Victor might. After all, there's not much difference between you and me."

"I don't guess there is. I don't guess there's a whole lot of difference between any two people."

"I wish you'd give in on this. You might not think it, but you never gave in to me on anything. I never led you anywhere, and I guess you were right. But maybe that was why we fought all the time. You may be better than me but you're not smarter than me. Still and all, I know you're not dumb. You don't need the land. And if it's Anne you're after, you can get her anyway."

I know I turned deep red.

Vance laughed, a rather pleasant laugh, and said, "A touch, a touch, I do admit! I don't blame you, Max. I like her looks myself."

He had almost won me over, because that unpredictable mind of his had touched a point which I thought no other mind could possibly reach. Sensing victory, he moved in again. "What do you say? I'll give you back five hundred dollars more than you gave me. What do you say?"

"I want to study about it."

"Listen to me. I don't want you to study about it. All I want is your word that you'll do it. I'll make a last offer: I'll give you a thousand dollars profit, and if that's not fair I can't make it fair. Now what do you say?"

"If Victor don't want it I might do it. I want to talk with him before I say."

"Victor doesn't want it. He had his chance. What does he know anyway? He's forty-four years old and got nothing but a houseful of kids."

"They happen to be pretty nice kids."

He was angry then, because he thought his victory was slipping away. "You wait and see. That girl will get you into trouble yet. You better . . ." Then he stopped. "Go on and talk to him. I imagine you'd stick your head in the fire if he said to."

He went on, and I had to go all the way back to Mr. Harmon's for the dogs. I was aggravated and tired of walking, and decided I was a smidgin dumb after all: a thousand dollars was a lot of money, which he might not offer again.

Most farmers can talk better, trade better, and give their best advice around the barn. So when Victor came home from Cross City in the afternoon I didn't tell him I had seen Vance; I waited until we went to feed. Even then, I kept putting off the subject as long as I could. I talked about the tombstones I had bought for Mama's and Rudy's graves. He asked about the beagle hounds which I had got from Mr. Harmon. I told him I wanted Carroll to have one and Claude the other. Then I asked him would it be all right if I got Claude a rifle for Christmas.

He said, "My goodness, that's too much of a Christmas present."

"It's not that," I explained. "It's whether you think he's old enough for one."

"Oh, I don't care. He's big enough. But that's too much of a present."

That matter was settled, very much to my satisfaction. I was looking forward to Christmas and the chance to give all of them something. I want to record here one of the strangest feelings I ever had: sometimes I would find myself almost wishing some misfortune would befall Victor or his family so I might show how much I could and would do for them. My mind was toying with the idea when I told Victor that Vance wanted the Big Springs place back.

"What did you tell him?" Victor acted unconcerned.

"I said I wanted to see you first. You might want it."

"If I don't want it, you aim to let him have it?"

"I thought I might. It's been their land for a long time. He said his daddy wasn't going to live long and he wanted it back. I wouldn't do it for Vance, but I may do it for Mr. Acroft. . . ."

"For Mr. Acroft . . ." Victor said, and he turned pale around his mouth. He was livid with anger; and I was all the more uneasy because I had never seen anything of the sort in him. "That boy is a liar, and I hate a liar! Don't you let him have a foot of that land. I got just a hint of something today. Somebody's trying to buy the land. He knows it and knows he can make something out of it. You let him sweat. He's a liar."

I was trembling, almost as if Victor had called me a liar. I said, "Victor, don't you think . . . sometimes a man *has* to lie?"

He turned on me. In his eyes was that cold annihilating stare, like Mr. Acroft's. "I don't want no kind of liar around me."

I was afraid of him then.

In the next two days, Vance came twice to see me, and both times we were off hunting. In the meantime we found out what was going on behind the curtain. A company wanted to buy the Big Springs place for some sort of dye factory, because of certain minerals in the spring water. There were plenty of rumors, as usual; people were guessing the company would pay ten or fifteen thousand dollars if it was handled right; and others said it was next thing to oil. It was understood there had been some dealings with Mr. Acroft a few years back and then the war had wiped out all plans; but now the company was interested again and would send a representative shortly. Word had leaked out through a letter to the Chancery Clerk's office. Of course, we had no way of knowing what was truth and what was rumor. There was nothing to do but wait.

On the morning of the thirteenth, Victor and I went to cut post for Mr. Harmon, who was building eighty rods of new fence across the lower side of his pasture. We went early hoping to get the posts cut in time to go hunting that afternoon. It was a damp, gray day and the cold seemed to sneak through our clothes until the saw warmed us.

We might have been through at noon but the second tree, a tall twenty-inch chestnut, lodged in the fork of a hickory.

"Let's leave it," I said. "He's got plenty more trees."

"No," Victor said. "Bad luck come a-knocking when you cut a tree and leave her be."

"Yes," I answered. "We try to cut that hickory and we're liable to get knocked on the head and fall down dead."

"We'll get it," he said, and I knew he wouldn't leave it like that if it took a year to get it on the ground.

He chipped the hickory and took the most dangerous position under the chestnut, and we worked slowly. Then as the hickory gave way we dropped the saw and broke clear. But I saw him stumble; his left foot had caught in a vine, and for a horrible second I thought he would be crushed. Then I saw he was clear of the chestnut, had been clear all the time, but he was bending over rubbing his knee. He limped to the stump and sat down.

"What's the matter?" I asked.

"Nothing. Just sorta jerked that old knee out of place."

I sat down with my back to Victor. I felt weak. I didn't want to think about his knee. We must have sat there silently for five minutes when I heard someone coming through the woods. It was Vance.

I got up and watched him approach. This time he did not seem pressed or nervous. When he came closer he called out rather good-naturedly, "Woodman, spare that tree!"

"You're too late," Victor said.

"No," Vance said. "I'm not too late. Am I, Max?"

I saw the cleverness in his eyes. He grinned and ran his fingers through his hair.

"I've heard you ought to go to the woods to trade with a woodman," he said.

Victor got up, as if we would go to work and Vance would have to leave. His knee obviously pained him.

"Cut a tree on yourself?" Vance said.

"Not hardly," Victor said. He started for the saw, but I went ahead of him.

When I returned with the saw, Vance had sat down. "You folks too busy to trade some?"

"I ain't got nothing to trade," Victor said.

Vance ignored the remark. His eyes seemed to be getting brighter all the time. He was looking at Victor's knee.

"You've heard about the dye factory. Might be something to it, might not. But you don't really want to keep that land, do you, Max?"

Victor was plainly out of humor. "Give me the saw," he said, roughly. He took his handle and stepped across the log. His face was twisted in pain.

"You're not answering much, are you?" Vance said.

"I thought I'd already answered," I said.

"A man could change his mind." He looked at Victor. "You know, Victor, I've been thinking about that knee of yours. I bet it gives you a lot of trouble."

"Don't worry about it."

"I didn't mean to make you mad," Vance said. "I was just trying to be friendly. Max understands that. In the first place, you should have been carried to Memphis instead of a one-horse hospital. They could've fixed it and you'd never have had any more trouble. And after all, the insurance company was paying. Besides, you could've sued them for plenty. I would have. But you . . . well, you're like Max. You're honest. You wouldn't take a penny that wasn't coming to you. Max wouldn't either. Would you, Max?"

He got up and walked off a few steps. I could see a strange sort of frown on Victor's face. Vance laughed. "You know, Victor, Max is going to think it over about a day, and then he's going to sell that land back to me. Because he's honest, like you. He's not out to make money off a dye factory . . . or say, an insurance company. . . ."

He walked off, leaving me and Victor looking at each other across the log.

"Crazy," Victor said.

I thought I wouldn't be able to pull the saw. I could feel sweat all over my body. "Maybe we better quit," I said, "if your knee . . . if . . ."

Victor bent down ready to work.

"Victor," I said, and I know he sensed the uneasiness in my voice. "I think I'll just sell him that land and get it over with."

He raised up. "You going crazy too? If you let him outtalk you now I'll kick your hind end all over these woods . . . with this crippled knee. I can't stand a liar."

4

EARLY, even before daylight, on the morning of the fourteenth, Victor and I went to help build the fence for Mr. Harmon. I had been awake most of the night with worries and questions crawling through my mind: If I gave in to Vance, how would I explain to Victor? If I did not give in, Vance would know what to do. (There in the darkness I could see the cleverness in his eyes.) I heard Miss Lillie when she got up in the night and fixed a salt poultice for Victor's knee.

I was glad when daylight came and we were on our way to the pasture. Victor did not limp very much, and he was in such a good humor that he lifted my spirits considerably. Later, I got such a laugh from the deep-post-hole idea that I forgot all my worries and felt the world perfectly in order again.

Mr. Harmon put us to digging the post holes while he hauled the posts. He was a little man, hard, quick, continuously busy, and not very talkative. He had to go a mile or more for the posts, hauling them twenty at a time over soggy ground. So we could dig the holes as fast as he could haul the posts and insert them. He would drive the wagon along the fence line, grab a post, rush to the hole, jab the post down with all his might, and then look at it as if it were not deep enough.

It was Victor's idea to dig a hole six feet deep. We did, while Mr. Harmon was gone for a load. We dug it six feet and six inches, deeper than the digger handles; and the water rose quickly, hiding the actual depth. Along came Mr. Harmon, rushed and solemn. He jabbed the post down and it went out of sight. He did not know what to think. He was actually scared. "I'll declare," he finally said. Not another word came out of him until eleven o'clock when he told me to take his pickup that afternoon and go to Cross City to get four rolls of wire, which he had already arranged for.

Victor said, "He's sending you because if he goes he

knows we'll laugh at him all the time he's gone. We ought
to be ashamed to do an old man like that."

"It was a mean trick," I agreed. Nevertheless, I was the
one who could not stop laughing, and felt Victor's idea was
the funniest simple thing I had ever seen.

After dinner I went for the wire and occasionally, as I
drove along, I laughed to myself over the picture of Mr.
Harmon jabbing a post out of sight. I got the wire, and when
I started out of the hardware store the storekeeper said, "I
know I'm not going to get the rifle you want before Christmas. But I've got a second-hand model just like it. You're
in such a good humor today I believe you'll buy it."

I turned back and spent five or ten minutes looking at the
rifle. Actually, I was trying to decide whether I wanted to
give Claude a second-hand gun, which I could have immediately, or whether I wanted to wait weeks, maybe months,
for a new one. "Take it and try it," he said. "I know the man
that owned it. It's practically a new gun because he never
used it. I'd give you the gun before I'd lie about it. The man
didn't like it because he had bad luck with it."

"What sort of bad luck?"

"Trouble with the game warden. The man's pretty bad to
hunt out of season. I think he got caught two or three times
and every time he got caught he had this gun. He just got a
notion it was unlucky. You know how things like that go.
But just between me and you, I'd rather have this gun than

a new one. It's prewar, and it's better material, and it's a real bargain, if you're not superstitious." He laughed heartily, and I rather liked him.

"But I am superstitious," I said.

"In that case, you'll have to pass up a bargain. And I wouldn't blame you. I'm a little that way myself. I guess everybody is to some extent. I heard an old feller not long ago talking along that line and he said men are a lot worse than women. I told him to hold on, but when I got to thinking about it, by George, I had to say he might be right. If you was to take it, you'd better get you a license."

"I don't want it for myself. I want it for a boy. A Christmas present."

"I wish Santa Claus would bring me a hundred like this. I could sell half of them tomorrow. But you suit yourself about this gun, son. If you want it though, you better get it today. Take it and try it two or three days. If you like it, pay me; if you don't, just bring the gun back."

"But you don't know me."

"No. But I know Vic Wells. Besides, I'll tell you something. I been in business thirty-one years and never lost a penny with a bad debt on a gun. It's a funny thing, folks will just naturally pay for a gun. I bet you didn't know that."

"No, I didn't know that."

"It's a fact. Course, I don't know about pistols. I never dealt with them. I'm talking about rifles and shotguns."

"I'll bet you're right."

"I know I'm right."

"I'm going to take the rifle," I said. I gave him a check. When he opened his cash register he took out four long cartridges and handed them to me.

"That's every one I got. There's not a box in the store. But I'll tell you what I'll do: I'll save you two boxes out of the next batch. I'll have some before Christmas I know."

I dropped the four into my shirt pocket, and thanked him. I felt rather good about the transaction, but hurried off, for I had lost a quarter hour of Mr. Harmon's time. There was in my mind a faint uneasiness: I did not like the idea of giving something for a present which was not brand new. I was not in the least superstitious, however, for I had forgotten that part of it.

I turned off the highway and followed an old field road to the corner of the pasture, or as close as the wet ground would allow. Neither Victor nor Mr. Harmon was in sight. I halloed two or three times but got no answer. Later, I learned that Mr. Harmon had mired the wagon down and Victor had gone to help him get out. Later, too, I was to say if I had not bought the second-hand rifle in the first place . . . if the storekeeper had kept his cartridges . . . if Mr. Harmon had not mired down . . . if Victor had been there . . . if . . . if . . . if . . .

If I had never been born . . .

I waited two or three minutes and then took the rifle, inserted the cartridges and shot twice at a sycamore ball in the top of a large sycamore, twenty or thirty yards away. I shook the ball each time but I did not knock it off. I put the safety on and stood the rifle against a sweet gum tree at the corner of the fence. I meant to have Victor shoot twice and see what he thought of the rifle.

I waited another two or three minutes and when no one was in sight I took the axe and cut a tamping stick for the posts. I came back to the gum tree and began to tamp the first post when I heard someone coming toward me. I gave one glance at the figure (which I thought was Victor) behind the hedge and went on tamping. The footsteps stopped, but still I kept on tamping, for I lacked only a few strokes having the dirt packed well around the corner post.

Then a voice said, "Are you too busy to talk to me, Harper?"

It was Vance. He had come through the hedge and was standing maybe twenty feet away.

"No. I'm not too busy."

He came to the post and shook it, as if to test how well I had tamped. I moved back and propped my foot against the gum tree.

"You got your trading clothes on?"

"Maybe," I said. "I made one trade today already."

He turned pale. His face jerked up and fixed on me. "Did you sell that land?"

"No."

"I want it."

"I know you want it."

"You're not going to be stubborn about it, are you?"

"No. I'm just going to keep it."

"You're not going to keep anything. I'll fix you! I can and I will and you know it. Don't you?"

"I know you'll try."

"Victor told you not to, didn't he?"

"Leave Victor out of it."

"Sorry. I can't. He's too involved. You'd do it if it wasn't for him. I know you're in a tight place. But it's better to break a window and crawl out the back than to stay in your glass house and let it crash on your head."

I stood looking at him. I knew again he would never stop, that something about me unnerved him, wore him raw. I began to feel a strange heaviness around my eyes, behind them.

"You're saying no?" His voice was quiet, almost peaceful; it was hardly a question.

"I'm saying no."

"I should have known you wouldn't do anything for me. You're like all the others, except you can read and write by some miracle of nature. After all we've done for you . . . to give you a chance. What have you got against me? Didn't we help you? If it hadn't been for my daddy, you'd be picking spinach in Arkansas, or digging fishbait in Tennessee, with a crooked foot. Listen, you think you're a landlord, but I think you're still what you were when you came here: a snotty-nosed, bare-footed, farm-hopping Shardy. But I know how to handle you. Just work on Victor. He's a Shardy and you're a Shardy and I'd be pretty dumb if I couldn't set you two against each other. Oh, I could tell him you're no good for his daughter. Or I could tell him you're a tookel. I could tell him anything. I could put lots of spiders in his mind. Only I won't. I'm too smart for that. I know exactly how to singe your feathers. Simply show Victor how you lied and cheated the insurance company—and him . . . your good friend. I've got all the facts, all of Papa's papers. When I get through, you'll lose more than Victor and his daughter. You'll be in the state penitentiary wishing you'd never had any Acroft land on your hands."

I was not mad. Through it all I never got mad. But the heaviness around my eyes went to my tongue. I could hardly speak.

"You wouldn't do it," I said.

"Why? Because of Papa? Because I'd get him in trouble too? Papa's going to die—a month, two months . . . It wouldn't hurt him. But when Victor finds out how honest you are . . ."

"Victor will understand. . . . I'll explain everything to him. . . . I'll . . ."

"Oh, no you won't. I'll put it to him in a clever way. You have to be clever, Max, to take care of your own interests. Like the time Papa ran you off. I didn't tell Papa what you think I told him. It had to be something extraordinary for him to run you off. You were practically heir apparent to the throne. So I told him you were Mr. ten Hoor's little sissy . . ."

I never took my eyes off him. I reached behind the sweet gum tree, felt the barrel against my fingers. It was so sudden he never moved. He was falling when I fired the second time. In the most peaceful voice he said, "Max . . . I really . . . liked you . . . all right. . . ." And then it seemed I could hear his tongue fall into silence.

I never moved from the tree. I leaned against it and felt a soft wind against my face. My body felt unusually large, not strong, not weak; and my left foot felt crooked, as in the old days. I looked down at my foot, and when I looked up again he was already blue. All I could think was: Well, it is finished. . . .

5

FROM the cell I watched the trains every day, and counted boxcars, and went over the whole story step by step. I was not sorry; or rather, I was not ashamed. I felt lowest early in the morning when the bells began in the church tower, which I could see rising in the mist, beyond a wholesale warehouse. Since the trial, even the bells do not bother me.

The county prosecuting attorney would not let me make bond. I made him mad when I refused to talk and he retaliated with all his power, which was enough. Although he didn't know it, I didn't want to make bond. I had no place to go. I could not go back to Victor's, and yet he would have expected it, for he is not one to turn his back on people, even when they are wrong. But I could not go back.

The only thing I had to hope for, I thought, was that Victor and Anne and the others would never know.

The trial was set for the January term of court. I had only two weeks to wait.

Two lawyers came to see me. I was nice to the first one because Victor had sent him. The second one came on his own hook and picked at me for an hour or two. I was all out of sorts, and finally yelled at him and said I didn't want a lawyer.

"What do you want?" he asked. "To hang by the neck until you're dead?"

"It's my neck."

"True. Unfortunately, however, you've got only one."

"I can count," I said.

"You may be able to count, but you're not able to reason very well. If we could prove he attacked you first . . ."

"I'm going to die, whatever you prove. Why should I lie or give you a lot of money to lie for me? I know what's going to happen to me."

The whole world had caved in, and it seemed to me it was

not worth the effort, even if I could have lifted everything with one finger. I wanted the trial to be finished, the sentence to rest on my head, and silence.

When the trial began at last, I thought I was ready. I thought: I will drive them out of their minds with my silence, for I am done with anyway. Suppose I said, "We were enemies from the beginning," or "He called me a tookel," or "He let Rudy die for him." It was better to tell nothing, absolutely nothing, for if I told one thing I might have to tell another; and at last they would find out the final thing that raised my gun.

The court appointed a lawyer for me. He was furious with me, and so was the jury and so was the judge; and the crowd was furious with disappointment. But for once in my life I stood above them; I was superior; I was the king. I was the only one in the world who knew. It fills you with a tremendous sense of strange power to be the only one in the world to know what the world is trying to find out. I made my speech quite clearly and not once faltered on a single word: "Yes, your Honor, something happened which has not been told. But as long as I live, I will never explain a single word of it. I am prepared to die."

I guess sooner or later I would have broken down, I would have told everything. But there in the huge and impressive courtroom I felt for the first time the power of the universe flow through me: it was like leaning back against a pine tree and feeling the cool wind, like vital strength, enter every pore of your body. After the first day, I even prayed that I would tell nothing. I would think: I am the only one in the world who knows what the world is trying to find out.

I was on the stand fourteen times. Three days of it. I was so tired I was sick at my stomach. They kept on and on, trying to get it out of me, as if they wanted an excuse to save me. I kept telling myself: You are not a fool; you are done with anyway; you can hold out; they want only to find out the secret and their appetites are whetted to the point of madness.

Contempt of court? "Do you understand the severity of such a charge?"

"I should imagine it is less severe, your Honor, than the penalty for murder."

The newspapers said I was brilliant. But sometimes, in the cell, with my face buried in the pillow, something told me I was a fool.

They must have decided I should win my empty victory. It was finished. I thought: Pity the poor people who came again and again and waited for me to break down and electrify them by unveiling the mystery. Yes, pity them; pity the ones who came to pick up the pieces which never fell apart. I breathe more easily, knowing it is done with, knowing the judge, like a god, has already said, "The gentlemen of the jury have reached a verdict of guilty. This court must therefore sentence you to die . . ."

I was the only one who heard, who really heard. For as

Mr. ten Hoor used to say, "If you have never bitten into the kernel of a peach seed how can you know the taste on your tongue?"

And so I came back to live until "four o'clock of the morning of the fourteenth of March." They may reduce me to zero but that is all. So far they have got nothing else. Strange, how people kept coming by, people whom I hardly knew or never knew at all, asking, "What really *did* happen?" As if I would suddenly pour out my heart to them.

Victor has not once asked. The other day I thought he might. He came in his overalls, for which I was thankful, and he sat on a stool just outside the bars and talked to me. The overalls, clean and well ironed, were right; if he had come in a tie and coat it would not have been the same at all. We could not have talked the full hour. I cannot put down many words that passed between us, but at the time I said to myself I must remember every syllable and set it down. I do remember watching the pockets on the bib of his overalls: his wife had ironed them so perfectly, so carefully. It was like a sermon, or music, or sunlight that reaches through my small window for a while each day. It is one thing I remember about my mother: she ironed so carefully. When I asked him about the family, I did not put Anne first. I deliberately put her last. Then he was gone and I lay on my cot and thought, Why did I do that? Why must we forever hide the truth? And a long time ago, why didn't I go to Victor and say: Victor, it was this way. Surely, Victor would have understood. But it is too late. All things are so simple in the end, when it is too late.

I was not surprised that Mrs. Acroft came. I felt a great loss when I saw her face was old, not Margo's; and I felt a certain relief too. She was old and broken. I had not seen her since before the war, and I had to keep looking to make certain I was not mistaken. "I must be humble," I thought. "She was his mother."

She sat down in the place provided. I came close to her, and looking through the bars, I said, "Mrs. Acroft."

She did not look directly at me. "I thought you wouldn't mind if I came by."

"I don't mind."

"I've not come to quarrel, or to condemn anybody. My son is gone and we can't bring him back. I want to talk, though. I just want to talk . . . and I want you to tell me some things. I always liked you, and Sidney did. I can't believe what's happened. It looks as if we're doomed. Sidney is coming home. He's given up now. He knows there's no chance for him. What have we done to bring all this down on our heads? Was Vance mean?"

"I don't know, Mrs. Acroft."

"He was a good child. Quiet. He read all the time. He was smarter than Margo, so much smarter! We loved him. We were good to him. But he never found anybody he loved; I'm sure he never found anybody. And it's better to love than to be loved, isn't it? Oh, I know it is."

Then she was quiet and I was quiet. There was almost no trace of emotion, merely a deep, unanswerable concern.

"You were wrong . . . you were wrong, but I can't believe you were *all* wrong. Years ago I hoped you would like each other. I hoped you would be friends. I would feel better if I only knew why. . . ." Then she looked directly at me for the first time. "Sidney was in school with the Governor. Oh, way back, at the University, and maybe he's forgotten. But you haven't much time. And maybe it would do no good anyway. If you would tell me your side of it . . . tell me why . . . I'll ask Sidney to go see him for you. I'll ask him to go, and he'll go. . . ."

Time went by us and I could hear it, a great stream out of nowhere and into nowhere. She was looking at me.

"Will you tell me?"

I shook my head. I said, "No," but whether it was loud enough for her to hear I can't say. I watched her rise slowly, felt her reach out and touch my fingers, which were curled around a bar. Without a word she went away.

I was torn to pieces. I was, for the first time, too weak to stand. I lay on my bunk and trembled. That was yesterday afternoon. All last night I said, "O God, there are only hours left now. Let it be done quickly."

This morning I felt better. When the jailer told me at breakfast that the executioner would begin to set up his equipment today, it did not seem to bother me. At last I know. It will be easy and painless. And I have much for which to be thankful: I have kept silent, I have remained reasonably strong, I have kept to the truth. I have known happiness and sadness; I have loved and been loved. I am so much dust, so much evil, so much good. I am not ashamed nor afraid. I am faintly curious to know what it is like to die.

I have great faith in something. What, I do not know. It may be I must die that another will be born. Back to the clay hills for a thousand or a million years. And then I shall be born again to live. Oh, I am not afraid, for there will be a few who will remember.

The time will come again. Though it is a million years, all things will pass, and those who judged me through a dark mirror will in turn be judged.

And, Vance, if we should meet in some yet unnumbered age, let me be forgiven.

Epilogue

ON THE morning of the thirteenth of March, twenty-four hours before Max Harper was scheduled to die, the State was without an executioner. Such a circumstance had not occurred during the lifetime of the Governor nor of the Governor's aides, who therefore went scurrying about to find a solution somewhere in black and white. The Governor issued a temporary reprieve.

In the meantime, the house of William Morgan was filled with newspapermen, not one of whom ever saw the original suicide notes. They were misplaced or hidden or destroyed, and the printed version of the "To whom it may concern" note was startlingly inaccurate, a mixture of several things in the mind of William Morgan's wife.

She gave the newspapers this account: "I cannot bring myself to execute an innocent man. I have seen many criminals, but I know this man is innocent as Jesus. I had rather lay down my own life than to take his."

Every daily paper in the State carried front-page, headline stories of William Morgan's suicide and reviewed Max Harper's case. Had the prisoner, by any chance, revealed his

secret to the executioner? Yes . . . every indication pointed
to such. And on and on the mystery grew. People stopped
on the street and held their hats in the March wind and said
it was odd indeed, and something should be done.

Telegrams and telephone calls poured into the capitol.

Then, on the fourteenth of March, at the urging of his
wife (if the prisoner lived she might someday learn his
secret), Sidney Acroft went to the capitol to see the Governor. He was an old man, broken, already intimate with death
and therefore eager to spare life, as if such a gesture would
add to his own days. It is only fair, however, to say that he
remembered many morning rides with the boy, remembered
all in a blue haze of standstill.

He pleaded earnestly with the Governor, and at last he
won a victory, which was to be kept secret for a while so it
would not appear the Governor had acted in too much haste.

A few weeks later, at seven o'clock in the evening, the
news of a pardon flashed across the wires. However, in order
to avoid publicity, Max Harper had gone free an hour earlier.

When he left the jail he had on the clothes he had worn
there (Victor had carried them home to be washed), and he
had under his arm a shirt box containing a few letters, his
last will and testament, and his manuscript. He walked
along the railroad for two or three miles and finally cut
across to the road which led to Victor's house. It was after
eight o'clock when he came into the yard and turned to his
left and stopped beside the chimney. He could hear the fire

and feel the warm rocks as he stood with his back to the chimney and looked inside. Each was occupied: reading, sewing, doing problems. Victor was oiling his shoes.

He watched for a few minutes and then he turned away. As he retraced his steps of a little while before, he occasionally looked back toward the house. When he came to the railroad he sat down and waited. The sudden and unusual exercise had made him weak and nauseated. When he stood up he was stiff.

He walked closer to town so the train, coming his way, would not have had time to gather speed. He could not wait until tomorrow, he could not wait to see anyone. Now, he must get away. But one day, when he was famous, when every schoolboy knew his name, when the evil cloud about him had blown away, he would come back to the ones he loved.

The train was long. Boxcar after boxcar went by slowly until he finally saw one with open doors moving toward him. He ran along the track, holding the shirt box in one hand and reaching out with the other.

As he leaped, he momentarily caught a vision of himself falling, his body torn and mangled, his left hand severed. Then he felt someone pulling at him and the next instant he was in the boxcar, prone, his face buried in straw. The little man squatting beside him said, "You near about didn't make it."

He raised his head briefly. He thought of his father. But then, the man was too small and his face was too old.

"Running away and ain't never coming back," the old man said.

He answered, "I don't know."

He was like one raised from the dead, without knowledge of what his direction might be tomorrow. He thought of Vance, and whether death could in any way be like trains tearing the night. He lay prone on the straw, his face buried. He did not want the old man to know he was crying.

About the Author

BORN ON 11 October 1922 on a farm near Corinth, Mississippi, Thomas Hal Phillips is the author of five published novels, several short stories, and numerous screenplays. His father, W. T. Phillips, was a farmer of English descent, while his mother, Ollie Fare Phillips, was a schoolteacher of Scotch-Irish descent. One of six children, Phillips attended Alcorn Agricultural High School near Corinth in Kossuth; there he played football, edited the school newspaper, and joined the debating team. After graduation, he enrolled at Mississippi State College, working his way through his first two years by drying "77,000,000 dishes," and, in his final two years, working at the YMCA. He majored in social science and participated on the debating team. He received his B.S. in 1943 and went immediately into the U.S. Navy. He served three years as a lieutenant (junior grade) with the amphibious forces in North Africa, Italy, and France. Part of this time he was a commander of an LC-1 and participated in the invasions of Anzio, Elba, and southern France.

Upon leaving the military, Phillips returned to college at the University of Alabama where he studied creative writing under Hudson Strode and Edward Kimbrough. In 1948, he received his M.A. As his thesis, he wrote a draft of *The Bitterweed Path*, which would become his first published novel. From 1948 to 1950, he taught creative writing in Dallas, Texas, at Southern Methodist University. Early in his career, Phillips was the recipient of several grants which allowed him to devote much of his time to writing: a Julius Rosenwald Fellowship in fiction in 1947, the Eugene F. Saxton Award in 1948, a Fulbright Fellowship for study in France in 1950, and in 1953 a Guggenheim Fellowship.

In 1958, he succeeded his brother Rubel Lex Phillips as Public Service Commissioner of the northern district of Mississippi. He served in this office until 1963 when he resigned to manage Rubel's gubernatorial campaign. Rubel, however, failed in his bid to be elected, and Thomas went into private business in Corinth and Jackson.

Since the sixties, Phillips has worked on a number of screen plays, as a consultant, author, or "screen doctor," and on several films in capacities other than writer. Among many films he has worked on are: *Tarzan's Fight for Life, The Brain Machine, Ode to Billy Joe, Minstrel Man, Walking Tall II, Huckleberry Finn, Nightmare in Badham County,* and *Roll of Thunder, Hear My Cry.* He worked on the Emmy award winning *Autobiography of Miss Jane Pittman,* and has been associated with Robert Altman's *Thieves Like Us, California Split, Nashville,* and *Buffalo Bill.* In *Nashville,* Phillips was the author of the "Hal Phillip Walker" segments after Altman directed him to invent a popular candidate—a man whom Phillips would like to see elected—and gave him no further limitations. Phillips himself recorded the speeches of "Hal Phillip Walker" for the soundtrack although the candidate's face was never seen in the film.

Despite his success in the motion picture industry, Phillips claims to be "more at home" with the novel. His first, *The Bitterweed Path,* was published in 1950, and deals, like most of his novels, with a young man's coming of age. The main character, Darrell Barclay, is the son of a failed share-cropper who becomes attached to Roger Pitt, the son of the successful owner of a cotton plantation. Darrell's father, a Ku Klux Klan night-rider, goes to work for Malcolm Pitt, Roger's father, and is later killed in Klan activities. The Pitts employ Darrell, but they come to love him as a member of the family. The novel mainly concerns itself with Darrell's adjustment over the years to his adopted family and to his relationship with Roger. The book traces Darrell's initial disorientation at the generous love of the Pitts to his gradual understanding and acceptance of it. As a first novel, *The Bitterweed Path* was generally well-received, garnering praise for its delicate touch and subtle restraint. The motivation was called "solid and good," although some portions of the book were considered unconvincing. As is usual in Phillip's work, place and time are evoked in a delicate and warm way. Critics particularly appreciated this aspect of his work and recognized Phillips as a promising new author with great control and sensitivity.

His second novel, *The Golden Lie*, published in 1951, dealt again with the growing up of a young boy, Foster Lloyd, and his friendship with another boy, Kirby. However, this novel injected the additional complications of race relations; Kirby is black. The boy's father helps coach the black school's football team and his mother is a "saint" in the local Primitive Church. As Foster moves toward maturity, he is shown moving away from his mother's religious views and gradually coming to a recognition of the hypocrisy inherent in the racially divided society. Kirby's possible future as a football player on scholarship is shattered when the church burns down and a benefit game is played between the white school and the black school. An angry fan kicks Kirby in the head after a hard collision between Foster and him, and Kirby dies. Although *The Golden Lie* was written with much of the same sensitive handling that characterized his first novel, critics considered the characters less complex and the theme less intricately worked out. The novel was praised for its subtle portrayal of family life in the South, but the book was not considered to be as emotionally intense as his first. Despite the explosiveness of his subject, even the brutality of Kirby's death is handled with a control that subdues the sensational possibilities in such a scene, perhaps diminishing its impact.

Search for a Hero, published in 1952, is Phillips' most critically successful novel to date. The central figure, Don Meadows, is a bright student whose accomplishments are not appreciated by his father or his brothers who are football players. The brothers, who can barely get through high school, abuse Don and force him to cheat for them on examinations so that they can go on to college. Don is completely isolated in his family, hating his brothers and father because of their insensitivity and ignoring his mother who is in a mental world of her own. Nonetheless, Don is also painfully aware of his father's desire for a heroic son and he talks his parents into signing the necessary papers for him to enlist. Once in the navy, Don continues to write themes for his brothers' freshman English so they can remain eligible to play football. He becomes part of an amphibious force that is sent to the Mediterranean and volunteers for a dangerous mission that turns into a fiasco. He is wounded in the escape from the area and returns home. He is treated with a certain awe and new respect by his family; however, he has matured and senses that his military heroism is nearly as meaningless as his brothers' gridiron exploits.

Most of the reviews of *Search for a Hero* praised Phillips' ear for dialogue, his humor, and handling of the theme. Again, he proved himself a subtle writer particularly interested in intrafamilial relationships. The central sections of the book, "A Man Called Victor," "Yosef the Tailor," and "Music of the Dead" are very well written. The bond between Yosef and Don is depicted particularly well. Phillips probably employed his own wartime experiences to recount Don's story; however, he skillfully avoids the melodrama and high seriousness of conventional war narratives. Although the war sections maintain a serious tone, Phillips weaves light and ironic touches throughout the text to illustrate his theme of the superficiality of most heroism. Phillips briefly touches on the issue of race relations when Don bunks near a black sailor, but it is not explored as deeply as it is in *The Golden Lie.*

In 1954, Phillips published *Kangaroo Hollow* in England. Because the book was never published in the United States, it has received little notice. Yet its intricacy of plot, its scope, and its complex themes perhaps make the book his most ambitious work. A large number of characters are examined closely, viewpoint is carefully shifted from character to character, and a large number of years go by. The central figure is Rufus Frost, a sharecropper who marries a moderately wealthy landowner and later goes into politics. Just as the United States enters World War I, Rufus marries Anna Shannon, despite their unequal social position and his passion for Todda. On the night that Anna gives birth to their first child, Rufus impregnates Todda. Rufus is drafted, along with several of the men from the Hollow, and although Anna's brother is murdered as the alleged father of Todda's child, Rufus is never exposed in the Hollow as the real father. Rufus survives the war and returns to run for sheriff in order to remove the stigma of having married into wealth. He enriches himself after winning the election by immediately becoming corrupted.

The final chapters of the book concern themselves mostly with the relationship among Rufus, Rex, and his intellectual brother Bayard. As in *Search for a Hero*, the intellectual brother feels an antagonism toward his football-playing brother, resenting his brother's recognition and apparent lack of character. Bayard becomes an activist writer and leaves the university after Rex, in a fit of anger, breaks Bayard's fingers. After this episode, Rex matures dramatically. He gives up a chance to play in the Sugar Bowl in order to return to his ill father's bedside. Later, as Rex runs for public office, he finds himself losing because of Bayard's sympathetic writing of Blacks and Rufus' proliquor record. Rex sees the emptiness of his football heroism, withdraws from the campaign with a speech adamantly defending the rights of Blacks. At the end of the novel, Rex, Bayard, and their father are drawn closer as the boys prepare to enter the Second World War.

Kangaroo Hollow explores many of Phillips' interests to some depth. Again he wrote primarily of the love-hate relationships inside families, of the antagonism between the intellectual and the more highly praised, physical individuals, and of the racial prejudice just beneath the surface of the society. Skillfully written, *Kangaroo Hol-*

low deserved much more recognition than it received. The trench warfare scenes are convincing and vivid, and the anguish of Howard (Jesse's murderer) is explored in detail. The scenes of Rufus with his sons on holidays are among the best of Phillips' portrayals of family life. *The Loved and the Unloved*, published in 1955, is Phillips' last published novel.

Not as well known as his novels or film scripts, several of Phillips' short stories received critical notice in the 1950s. "The Shadow of an Arm" (*Virginia Quarterly Review*, 16 [1950], 578-86) was among the O. Henry Prize Stories of 1951. "A Touch of Earth" (*Southwest Review*, 34 [1949], 340-47) was included in the Martha Foley *Best American Short Stories of 1949*. In 1952, "Lone Bridge" (*Southwest Review*, 36 [1951], 104-10) was listed in the Martha Foley "Roll of Honor." "Mostly in the Fields" (*Virginia Quarterly Review*, 27 [1951], 546-55) became part of *Search for a Hero*. An interview with Phillips was published in the spring 1973 issue of *Notes on Mississippi Writers*, pp. 3-13.

JAMES M. DAVIS, JR.

From *Lives of Mississippi Authors, 1817-1967*,
ed. James B. Lloyd (Jackson: University
Press of Mississippi, 1981)

gonnect.
vzw.
btgewice.com